Yes Indeed

Tales from Yes without Jon Anderson

by

Preston M. Frazier

Yes Indeed

DEDICATION

To the '5% for something fans'.

To the dreamers, the seekers, and the soundscapers—

This book is dedicated to those who find magic in melodies of the world's greatest progressive rock band, and courage in creativity, and meaning in every note. To the artists who shape our hearts with their craft, and the fans who carry their legacy forward—this is for you.

ACKNOWLEDGEMENT

Thanks to all the Yes fans, and especially the *5% for Something* fanatics. This book represents a history of the band I love. Of course, there are many great books out there about the "world's greatest progressive rock band." These are simply my thoughts about an unusual period in that history.

Special thanks to the *Slang of Ages* podcast supporters and patrons: Cheryl Frazier and Cynthia Tom. Thanks also to Joe Williams for his years of support, and to Rolando Guzman for both his support of the podcast and his outstanding cover design for this book, as well as for Toto: *The Band, Not the Dog.* Front and back cover artwork is also by Rolando Guzman.

Thanks to *Projekt Gemineye* leader and Yes expert Mark Anthony K, and to the *Yes Music Podcast.* I'm also grateful to the supporters of *slangofages.com*, including Monica Mitchell, Susan Frazier, and Something Else Reviews.com.

Thank you to Yes' Billy Sherwood for answering my persistent questions!

A very big thanks to Vinicio Cifuentes for his infinite patience and unwavering support.

TABLE OF CONTENT

INTRODUCTION

In a dimly lit London club called La Chasse, amidst smoky air and the sound of distant conversation, two musicians met by chance. It was April of 1968. Jon Anderson, a quiet man with a clear voice and dreams larger than the small clubs he performed in, found himself in deep conversation with Chris Squire, a tall bassist with thoughtful eyes and a passion for musical experimentation. Jack Barrie, who owned the club and often brought artists together, had introduced them, sensing their musical paths should cross. London's music scene thrived on moments like these—simple, unplanned meetings that sparked powerful creative partnerships.

Both Anderson and Squire quickly discovered a shared appreciation for intricate vocal harmonies. Their musical tastes overlapped remarkably, inspired profoundly by groups like Simon & Garfunkel and The 5th Dimension. This mutual admiration for layered vocals soon became a foundational element of their music. Not long after their initial meeting, they gathered at Squire's modest home to write their first collaborative song, "Sweetness." The synergy was immediate, natural. The ease with which they crafted this song hinted that they had stumbled upon something extraordinary.

At that time, Chris was playing bass in a psychedelic band named Mabel Greer's Toyshop. This ensemble included guitarist Peter Banks, guitarist and singer Clive Bayley, and drummer Robert Hagger. Jon Anderson's addition to this group gave him and Squire further opportunities to explore their evolving ideas on stage. Their performances at legendary clubs like The Marquee and UFO Club provided valuable experience and exposure, yet both Anderson and Squire sensed a deeper potential awaiting exploration beyond the constraints of Mabel Greer's Toyshop.

Peter Banks, who knew Chris from their earlier band, The Syn, soon rejoined after briefly playing with Neat Change. Banks' return came with a new sense of purpose; he suggested renaming the band "Yes" and even took on the task of designing their very first logo. His contributions solidified their emerging identity, making him integral to their early development. The arrival of Tony Kaye further enriched the band's sonic landscape. Kaye, a classically trained keyboardist with significant jazz influences, provided depth and complexity to their compositions, filling their sound with atmospheric layers.

Yet, despite this growing synergy, something crucial was still missing—a drummer whose rhythmic sensibilities could bind these disparate musical threads together. This need led to Bill Bruford responding to an advertisement they placed in Melody Maker. Bruford, deeply influenced by jazz rhythms and known for his technical skill, brought complexity and sophistication to the group. After auditioning in the basement of the Lucky Horseshoe Café, it became clear that he was precisely what Yes required. With Bruford's arrival, the band's original lineup was finally complete.

Yes had ambitious musical goals from the beginning. They did not wish merely to emulate popular music but sought to forge their own innovative path. Jon Anderson described their early aspirations as aiming to be "poppy but not doing Top 10 stuff," signaling a desire to appeal broadly while maintaining creative independence. Their unique vision combined elements of classical melodies, television themes, and rock—a distinctive fusion influenced by bands like Vanilla Fudge and The Beach Boys. Their sound was distinctive, complex, and decidedly ambitious.

Their creative process emphasized collaboration and improvisation. Jon Anderson directed melodies and lyrics, often guiding the overall vision of each composition. Chris Squire, with his innovative bass playing, crafted memorable lines that functioned almost as a second lead instrument. Bill Bruford's rhythms, drawn from jazz, introduced spontaneity and complexity to their arrangements. Tony Kaye's keyboard provided harmonic structure, contributing essential emotional dimensions to their songs. They developed their compositions organically, through extensive jamming and experimentation, assembling their music piece by piece.

Their debut album, titled simply Yes, boldly showcased their innovative style. This record featured ambitious reinterpretations of existing songs. For instance, their cover of The Beatles' "Every Little Thing" dramatically transformed a straightforward pop tune into a lengthy, expansive exploration of psychedelic rock. Tracks like "Looking Around" highlighted Chris Squire's prominent melodic bass playing, and songs such as "Harold Land" hinted at the ambitious compositions they would later perfect. The album was an ambitious first statement, marking Yes as a band willing to challenge conventional rock music.

Critics initially responded favorably. Rolling Stone praised their debut, describing it as "a definitive album." Early performances also sat well with audiences, particularly a memorable show where Yes filled in unexpectedly for Sly and the Family Stone. This performance notably impressed Roy Flynn, who soon became their manager, helping the band navigate the complexities of the music business. Their artistic journey had truly begun.

Despite early success, Yes faced its first significant challenges when Bill Bruford temporarily left to pursue academic studies. Tony O'Reilly briefly replaced him, but struggled to match the intricate rhythms required by the group's complex arrangements. Fortunately, Bruford returned in time for Yes to open for Cream at their farewell concert at the Royal Albert Hall—a significant milestone that solidified their emerging reputation.

Peter Banks soon encountered creative differences, departing just after the recording of their second album, Time and a Word. He opposed integrating orchestral elements into their sound, a decision that marked Yes's willingness to continually evolve, even at the expense of losing original members. Steve Howe stepped in as Banks' replacement, symbolically appearing on the album cover although he didn't perform on the recording. Howe's arrival signaled a critical new phase, promising greater innovation and expansion.

Throughout these shifts, the partnership between Jon Anderson and Chris Squire remained steadfast, forming the enduring core of Yes. Anderson, as the visionary leader, and Squire, with his distinctive musicianship, provided stability through changing lineups and musical directions. Their collaboration ensured continuity, even as other band members came and went.

Yes's journey became emblematic of constant evolution, courage in musical experimentation, and resilience amid change. Their beginnings—an ordinary meeting in a London club—grew into a narrative of transformation and discovery, with each challenge refining their collective identity. Their musical innovations not only shaped their sound but also reflected universal themes of growth, adaptation, and the pursuit of creative excellence. This first chapter was only the starting point for a band determined to push beyond conventional boundaries, forever moving forward.

CHAPTER 01
THE UNLIKELY MAGIC OF 'DRAMA'

In the autumn of 1980, as dusk settled over London's foggy streets, the air carried a secret promise of change—a promise that the familiar might yet be reborn. For Yes, a band long defined by its intricate progressions and sprawling epics, that night was the quiet prelude to a transformation both unexpected and inevitable. The stage was set not in a grand arena but in the collective determination of its members—a determination that, despite internal fractures and the loss of cherished icons like Jon Anderson and Rick Wakeman, the creative spirit of Yes would not only endure but evolve.

The departure of Anderson and Wakeman had rattled the core of the band, shaking the foundations of what many believed was the only possible identity of Yes. In the wake of long, sometimes fractious sessions in Paris, where creative visions clashed like tempestuous storm fronts, the remaining trio—guitarist Steve Howe, bassist Chris Squire, and drummer Alan White—stood at a crossroads. There was an air of disillusionment, of bitter memories of missed cues and fractured collaborations, yet within that very disarray glimmered the possibility of reinvention. It was a moment where loss and longing intermingled with the hope of forging a new sonic path.

Into this uncertainty stepped Trevor Horn and Geoff Downes, fresh from the bright, pulsating world of The Buggles. Their arrival was unexpected, a merging of worlds that had hitherto existed in parallel universes. Horn's voice, with its unique timbre and robust clarity, hinted at echoes of the past while boldly charting its own course. Downes brought with him a modern sensibility—a palette of synthesizers and digital textures that whispered of futuristic soundscapes. Together, they infused Yes with a spirit of audacity, challenging the notion that progressive rock could not adapt to the times.

In the studio, the atmosphere was electric. The recording sessions became a charged canvas where each note and nuance was painted with a fervor born of both nostalgia and anticipation. As Steve Howe laid down his aggressive, machine-gun-like guitar licks on the opening track, "Machine Messiah," the very air seemed to vibrate with possibility. His Gibson ES 345 roared through the speakers, each riff a testament to his reinvigorated passion—a fierce contrast to the more measured, classical approach of earlier years. Chris Squire's bass, thick and resolute, carved out a counterpoint that was both haunting and affirming. Alan White's drumming, crisp and impeccably precise, underscored the track with a heartbeat that matched the urgency of the times.

"Machine Messiah" was more than a song—it was a sonic manifesto. The interplay between Horn's and Squire's call-and-response vocals lent the track an almost ritualistic quality, a dialogue between past legacies and future promise. The swirling synthesizer passages from Downes were not mere ornaments but vivid strokes of color that illuminated the musical narrative. It was as if the band had reached into its own storied past and, with trembling yet determined hands, reassembled the shattered pieces into a new mosaic. In that moment, Yes redefined what it meant to be Yes—steeped in tradition yet daringly forward-looking.

Not long after the reverberations of "Machine Messiah" had settled, the album's next movements unfurled with a delicate balance of reflection and defiance. "Man In A White Car" emerged like a spectral interlude—a brief, almost dreamlike passage that stirred the imagination. The sparse yet evocative lyrics, paired with the unmistakable timbre of a Fairlight synthesizer, evoked images of a solitary figure drifting along an urban skyline. In the cool blue light of a late evening, the song's orchestral passages—tinged with the haunting echoes of timpani and snare—seemed to capture both the beauty and the melancholy of an era in flux.

As the record continued its journey, "Does It Really Happen" burst forth with a kinetic energy that belied its origins. Born out of the ashes of the aborted Paris sessions, the song was a declaration of resilience. The layered interplay between Steve Howe's rhythmic guitar sweeps and Geoff Downes' innovative keyboard textures created a sound that was both familiar and daringly new. Chris Squire's bass work shone through as the backbone of the track—a constant, pulsing reminder of the band's enduring heartbeat. Here, Trevor Horn's vocal delivery was measured and intense, his multi-tracked harmonies spoke of hope amid uncertainty. In every bar, every pause, Yes was quietly asserting its right to transform without erasing its legacy.

In the reflective space of the studio, the band's camaraderie was palpable. There was an unspoken understanding among them—a shared belief that music was not simply a product of individual prowess, but a collective, living entity that grew stronger through collaboration and reinvention. Even as tensions from the past lingered like shadows in the corners of the room, each member found solace in the act of creation. They were artists bound by a commitment to push boundaries, and in doing so, they began to craft not just an album, but a narrative of redemption.

"Into The Lens" captured this new chapter with a gentle yet insistent urgency. It was the sole single released from the album, and while it did not ascend to the heights of chart-topping success, its layered complexity and understated power were undeniable. The track's interplay of choppy basslines, techno-inspired keyboards, and Steve Howe's steel guitar evoked a sense of introspection—a moment of pause amidst the fervor. Trevor Horn's tenor, plaintive yet determined, lent the song a quality of quiet resilience. It was as if the band, through this song, invited its listeners to look deeply into the reflective surfaces of memory and change, to witness the subtle alchemy of loss transforming into innovation.

The narrative of transformation continued to unfold on "Run Through The Light." Here, the rhythmic pulse of a plucky acoustic guitar intertwined with the skittering cadence of piano and drums, creating a soundscape that was both intimate and expansive. In the interplay of these sounds, there was a sense of vulnerability—a fleeting recognition that even in their boldest moments, the band's journey was a fragile, unfolding story. Trevor Horn's vocal delivery here was marked by a controlled power, a deliberate choice to infuse each note with an emotional clarity that spoke to the struggles and triumphs of the moment. Meanwhile, Chris Squire's adventurous foray into the realm of the grand piano added an unexpected depth, blurring the lines between rock's raw edge and the tender subtleties of a bygone era.

Then came "Tempus Fugit," the album's closing track, which stood as both a culmination and a new beginning. The title itself—a Latin phrase meaning "time flies"—echoed the bittersweet passage of years, capturing the relentless forward march of time and change. As the track unfurled, it became a sonic odyssey, with Steve Howe's blistering guitar work slicing through the atmosphere like shards of light through a stormy sky. Chris Squire's bass, rich and resonant, carried the melody with an assurance that belied the tumultuous history behind each note. The expansive keyboard passages, the fervent vocals of Trevor Horn, and the dynamic interplay of each instrument coalesced into a rousing declaration of resilience. It was a track that encapsulated the band's ability to adapt—to absorb the shocks of loss and emerge with a sound that was both radically transformed and intimately familiar.

Yet, for all its bold experimentation and modern edge, the journey of 'Drama' was also one of quiet, personal evolution. Each band member, from the ever-dedicated Chris Squire to the visionary Steve Howe, found themselves in a process of rediscovery. In the dim glow of recording sessions and the reflective solitude of late-night rehearsals, they were not merely reinventing their music; they were reimagining their very identities. The new roles they embraced did not signify a rejection of the past but rather a respectful nod to it—a commitment to honor the legacy of Yes while daring to dream of what could be.

As the album made its way into the ears of fans and critics alike, initial reactions were mixed. There were whispers of dissent, echoes of disbelief from those who held fast to the memory of Jon Anderson's ethereal vocals and Rick Wakeman's majestic keyboards. Yet, as the years passed, perceptions began to shift. The very qualities that had once been viewed as departures from tradition came to be seen as the raw materials of reinvention. Listeners, much like the band itself, began to recognize that 'Drama' was not a mere aberration but a vital chapter in Yes's storied evolution—a period when vulnerability met ambition, and skepticism yielded to a slow-burning appreciation.

By the time the band finally returned to the live stage in later years, performing the album in its entirety, the cultural conversation had transformed. What was once underappreciated had blossomed into a cult classic, celebrated for its audacity and its beautiful, if unconventional, fusion of old and new. 'Drama' had become emblematic of the band's resilience, a reminder that true artistry often lies in the willingness to take risks, to embrace change, and to find magic in the most unlikely of places.

Standing on the precipice of change, Yes had redefined itself not through a return to what had been, but by boldly stepping into the unknown. Their journey through 'Drama' was a testament to the enduring power of reinvention—a musical comeback story that was as much about the evolution of sound as it was about the evolution of spirit. In the interplay of vibrant synthesizers, the raw intensity of guitar, the steadfast pulse of the bass, and the unyielding drive of the drums, there emerged a new Yes—a band that had transformed its drama into a new kind of magic.

And so, beneath the muted glow of studio lights and the watchful eyes of time, Yes crafted an album that would quietly reverberate through decades—a work of art that captured the transient beauty of change, the poetry of loss and renewal, and the ineffable resilience of the human spirit. In 'Drama,' every note, every pause, every whispered phrase told the story of a band reborn, a story that continues to echo in the hearts of those willing to listen to its unlikely magic.

CHAPTER 02
INTO THE STORM – EXPLORING 'FLY FROM HERE'

In the dim light of early morning studio sessions, as the hum of equipment blended with the distant clatter of city life, Yes gathered once again at the precipice of transformation. The air was cool and charged with an anticipation that felt almost electric, as if every note waiting to be played carried the weight of the band's storied past and the promise of a brave new future. In those moments, "Fly From Here" was more than an album—it was a journey through turbulent skies, a reflective chronicle of internal struggles, creative reinventions, and the enduring desire to produce music that remained both relevant and transcendent.

For Yes, the path to "Fly From Here" was strewn with challenges and moments of quiet revelation. The late 2000s had brought seismic shifts to the band's lineup and identity. When longtime vocalist Jon Anderson's presence was sidelined by health concerns, the band took a courageous leap by inviting Benoît David—a singer whose roots ran deep in the tradition of Yes—to step into a role once thought impossible to fill. This change, along with the return of keyboardist Geoff Downes, who replaced Oliver Wakeman and carried with him memories of the band's 1980 "Drama" era, set the stage for a narrative that was as much about survival and adaptation as it was about artistic expression.

It was during a late-night conversation between bassist Chris Squire and producer Trevor Horn that the seed of "Fly From Here" was first nurtured. In a quiet corner of a Los Angeles studio, amid scattered sheet music and the lingering aroma of strong coffee, they rediscovered a long-dormant idea—a demo written by Horn and Downes in the pre-"Drama" days. That demo, a gentle whisper of what could be, had been performed live decades ago by a now-legendary lineup. Yet, it had never been fully realized in a studio, waiting patiently for its moment. With renewed determination, the band resolved to expand this spark into an epic suite, a centerpiece for an album that would navigate both familiar landscapes and uncharted territories.

The recording sessions, split between Los Angeles and London, were both a reunion and a reinvention. In the recording booth, voices merged with instruments in a dance of creativity and conflict. Benoît David, whose French-Canadian accent lent a unique texture to his delivery, was guided meticulously by Horn—a man who, having once worn the mantle of lead vocalist himself on the "Drama" album, knew intimately the stakes of reclaiming a storied legacy. Downes's keyboards, layered with precision and emotion, set a gentle but insistent pulse that reminded everyone present of the band's musical roots. And then there was Steve Howe, whose nimble fingers on the guitar evoked memories of a bygone era while pushing the instrument into new, unanticipated territories.

At the heart of the album lay the "Fly From Here Suite"—a nearly 25-minute odyssey divided into six parts that captured the full spectrum of Yes's musical and emotional journey. The suite opened with an "Overture" that unfolded like the soft, first light of dawn. Geoff Downes's piano notes, distant yet resonant, floated through the studio like whispered secrets. Each repeated theme grew in intensity, like the slow gathering of clouds before a storm, until the entire band joined in with punctuated chords that announced the arrival of something momentous. This opening segment was an invitation—a delicate prologue that hinted at the grand narrative to come.

As the suite flowed into "Part I: We Can Fly," a driving bass line and the introduction of Benoît David's vocals signaled a departure from the quiet introspection of the overture. It was as if the band had gathered its collective strength and taken flight, propelled by a desire to soar beyond the confines of past limitations. The music here was both uplifting and determined, capturing the feeling of stepping out into a wide-open sky after a long period of confinement. It was a musical embodiment of ambition—a promise that, despite the internal turbulence and external challenges, Yes would rise.

"Sad Night at the Airfield" was the next chapter in the suite—a section that transported the listener to a lonely airfield under a moonlit sky. Here, Steve Howe's acoustic guitar intertwined with rhythmic percussion and subtle keyboard textures, creating an atmosphere of cinematic melancholy. In the background, a delicate vocal line emerged, one that David picked up with a poignant sensitivity. Chris Squire's bass provided gentle, well-placed touches that underscored the inherent sadness, like soft footfalls on a deserted runway. This movement was not merely a musical interlude; it was a moment of introspection—a space where the band allowed themselves to feel the weight of past regrets and the bittersweet nature of change.

The suite then shifted gears with "Part III: Madman at the Screens." In this section, the tension of the narrative crystallized into a burst of kinetic energy. Steve Howe's guitar, now wilder and more aggressive, danced erratically against a backdrop of pounding drums and pulsating keyboards. It was a section that evoked images of flickering screens and the relentless pace of modern life—a mad, chaotic moment where the struggle between order and disarray became almost palpable. Yet even in the chaos, there was an underlying unity— a testament to the band's ability to harness disorder and mold it into something powerful.

"Part IV: Bumpy Ride" provided a stark contrast to the preceding turbulence. As the title suggests, the music here mimicked the uneven cadence of a rough journey. The intricate interplay between Steve Howe's rhythmic guitar lines and the dynamic contributions of Chris Squire's bass evoked the image of a stunt team performing a precision act, navigating obstacles with synchronized brilliance. Despite the occasional jolt and unexpected shift, the passage was executed with a meticulous precision that belied its erratic nature—a true whirlwind of sound that reflected the band's turbulent but powerful synergy.

Finally, the suite reached its conclusion in "Part V: We Can Fly (Reprise)." This section was a triumphant return to the theme that had been set at the beginning of the journey. The reprise gently reintroduced the familiar melodic line of "We Can Fly" just as it seemed to fade away, as if to remind the listener that even after the wildest storm, there is always the possibility of calm and renewal. Benoît David's vocal delivery, imbued with both strength and vulnerability, lent the final chorus an almost cathartic quality. Chris Squire's climbing bass line built a sense of momentum, carrying the music forward before it slowly faded into a reflective silence. The suite, in its entirety, was not merely an arrangement of songs—it was a narrative arc, a sonic biography of Yes, with each movement capturing a facet of the band's evolving identity.

While the "Fly From Here" suite stood as the album's epic centerpiece, the other tracks on the album unfolded like individual vignettes—each a snapshot of personal and collective struggles, victories, and introspections.

"The Man You Always Wanted Me to Be" emerged as a tender ballad that veered unexpectedly from the grandeur of the suite. Written in the early 2000s by Chris Squire and Gerard Johnson, with lyrical contributions from Simon Sessler, this song was a deeply personal statement—a gentle exploration of identity and expectation. In its measured pace, the track allowed Squire's voice—a lead vocal delivered with a rare, earnest timbre—to convey an intimate narrative. Light conga touches by session player Luis Jardim and the delicate piano by Gerard Johnson added textures that evoked the soft patter of rain on a quiet afternoon. Subtle shifts in time signature, explained through a metaphor of a winding road that unexpectedly twists and turns, made the song's progressive elements accessible to any listener. Steve Howe's electric guitar, as fluid and intricate as ever, wove in and out of the melody, grounding the song in the unmistakable Yes sound. The track was a reflection on what it meant to both be and aspire—a lyrical and musical inquiry into the selves the band members had known and the selves they hoped to become.

"Life on a Film Set" offered a different kind of narrative—a series of vivid, almost dreamlike impressions. In its original version, the song opened with the gentle strumming of Steve Howe's Spanish guitar, its notes warm and inviting as if recalling the golden hues of an old cinema. Geoff Downes's orchestral keyboard touches provided a lush, cinematic backdrop, evoking images of bustling film sets and the ephemeral magic of captured moments. As the pace quickened, the lyrics began to paint a tapestry of vivid imagery—brief flashes of color, sound, and emotion that evoked the surreal quality of life under the limelight. Chris Squire's harmonies and Alan White's steady, pulsating drumming added a sense of continuity and urgency, as though every instrument were striving to capture a fleeting moment of artistic brilliance before it slipped away. Though the song was over before one could fully settle into its world, it left behind a lingering sense of wonder—a promise that the art of storytelling through music was as potent as ever.

"Hour of Need" was a song born of its own series of transformations—a piece that had evolved through myriad versions before finding its place on "Fly From Here." Originally a Steve Howe composition featured on his 2005 solo album under the title "In the Hour of Need," the track underwent metamorphosis when reimagined by the full band. On this version, Benoît David's vocals, supported by Howe's plaintive acoustic guitar passages, imbued the song with a raw urgency that spoke of social injustice and the need for change. The interplay of Geoff Downes's brief, emotive synthesizer solo with the gentle strumming of the acoustic guitar was like the interplay of shadow and light—each moment a reflection of struggle and hope intertwined. In a later, extended version known as "Fly From Here – The Return Trip," the song was given an even more expansive treatment: a soaring Asia-like electric guitar introduction heralded its arrival, and a superfluous instrumental coda rounded out its narrative arc. Each version of "Hour of Need" was a testament to the band's willingness to revisit and rework their creations—constantly seeking to refine their message and their sound.

Then there was "Solitaire," a pure and unadorned showcase of Steve Howe's virtuosic guitar artistry. In this solo piece, Howe seamlessly blended classical, flamenco, and country influences into a joyous, fingerpicked celebration of musical freedom. The piece was reminiscent of the delicate yet intricate compositions of Chet Atkins— a journey through a landscape of gentle arpeggios and soulful licks. In "Solitaire," every note was deliberate, every pause significant—a reflective interlude that stood as a quiet counterpoint to the expansive epics elsewhere on the album. It was a moment of introspection, a solitary flight of fancy that encapsulated the essence of Howe's creative spirit.

"Into the Storm," the final full-length song on the album, served as a powerful, multifaceted coda to the journey. This track was a reminder that even as one weathered the turbulence of change, there remained the steady pulse of life and creativity at its core. Layered with multiple time signatures and buoyed by a lead vocal performed by the Yes choir, "Into the Storm" wove together acoustic piano, organ, and synthesizer parts—a collaboration featuring contributions from Geoff Downes, Oliver Wakeman, and others. The song's bass-driven foundation, courtesy of Chris Squire's signature style, provided a rhythmic anchor amid the swirling, kaleidoscopic interplay of guitars and keyboards. Benoît David's assured vocal performance lent the chorus an air of resolute optimism—a declaration that despite the challenges and the shifting dynamics, Yes could still produce music that was both accessible and progressive. Alan White's masterful navigation of the time changes, executed with an understated yet vibrant energy, ensured that the song moved with a life of its own. "Into the Storm" was a testament to the band's enduring vitality—a final, stirring exclamation that the spirit of Yes was as much about persistence and evolution as it was about musical innovation.

Rounding out the album's narrative—and offering a stark contrast to the soaring optimism of "Into the Storm"—was "Don't Take No For an Answer," a track featured on the "Fly From Here – Return Trip" version. In this song, Steve Howe's composition incorporated his signature fingerpicked acoustic style alongside a prominent bass melody from Chris Squire. Yet despite these familiar hallmarks, the song felt at times disjointed—hampered by underwhelming keyboard textures and a vocal performance that, while earnest, failed to ignite the spark found elsewhere on the album. It was a reminder that not every creative risk pays off, and that even within a band as accomplished as Yes, there are moments when the storm clouds linger a little too long.

Behind the layered harmonies and intricate time signatures, there lay a story of conflict, adaptation, and ultimately, collaboration. The process of making "Fly From Here" was as much about reconciling internal struggles as it was about crafting a masterpiece. The band's shifting dynamics were palpable—a blend of old wounds and new alliances, where the legacy of Yes's past converged with the ambitions of its present. Benoît David, thrust into the role of lead vocalist in the absence of Jon Anderson, faced the daunting challenge of stepping into shoes that had long been revered. His journey was one of quiet determination—a journey that involved countless hours of vocal coaching under Trevor Horn's vigilant guidance, sessions where the nuances of English pronunciation and the subtleties of Yes's lyrical traditions were painstakingly honed. In these moments, the studio became both a sanctuary and a crucible—a place where the pressures of legacy met the heat of innovation.

Geoff Downes's return to the keyboard was similarly charged with meaning. Having been a vital part of the band's "Drama" era, his presence on "Fly From Here" was a deliberate nod to a time when Yes had already proven its ability to reinvent itself. Downes's keyboards provided a bridge between eras—a sonic continuity that connected the past with the present. His interplay with Trevor Horn, whose production legacy included monumental successes like "90125" and "Big Generator," reinforced the notion that the creative energy of Yes was not confined by time but was ever-evolving.

Steve Howe and Chris Squire, the enduring pillars of the band, found themselves navigating these turbulent currents with a measured grace. Howe's guitar work, whether it was the fiery solos of the "Fly From Here" suite or the tender strains of "Solitaire," remained as innovative as ever—a blend of raw passion and meticulous craftsmanship. Squire's bass lines, ever the melodic backbone of Yes, resonated with a sense of purpose. Their contributions were not merely technical feats but were imbued with the lived experiences of a band that had weathered countless storms.

In the midst of these creative negotiations, the studio became a microcosm of the band's internal landscape—a place where moments of quiet collaboration mingled with bursts of frenetic energy. It was here, in that crucible of sound and emotion, that the songs of "Fly From Here" were forged. The technical complexities—shifting time signatures that mimicked the unpredictable nature of a turbulent storm, layered harmonies that soared and intertwined like birds in flight—were rendered accessible through metaphors that spoke to everyday experience. The music was described as a whirlwind of sound, a dynamic interplay of light and shadow that captured the band's turbulent yet powerful synergy. In these moments, the technical became poetic, and every chord progression or rhythmic shift was a chapter in the greater narrative of Yes.

"Fly From Here" was not simply an album released into the ether of the modern music scene; it was a deliberate act of storytelling—a narrative that paid homage to the past while boldly charting a course for the future. The recurring themes of flight and journey, so evident in the album's title and the central suite, served as enduring metaphors for change, liberation, and the ceaseless quest for reinvention. The lyrics evoked images of airfields bathed in twilight, of radar screens flickering with messages of hope and warning—a reminder that every journey, no matter how fraught with turbulence, holds the promise of a new beginning.

Critically, "Fly From Here" was met with a spectrum of responses. While some listeners were captivated by the album's ambitious scope and the seamless blend of old and new, others found themselves hesitating—unsure if the absence of the familiar could ever be fully reconciled with the band's storied legacy. Yet, as is often the case with transformative art, time has a way of softening initial resistance. Over the years, the album has grown in stature, embraced not only as a relic of the past but as a vibrant expression of the band's enduring spirit.

For those who listened deeply, the album revealed itself as a multifaceted document—a record of a band in constant dialogue with itself. The "Fly From Here" suite, with its sweeping movements and intricate transitions, captured the grand ambition of Yes, while individual tracks like "The Man You Always Wanted Me to Be" and "Solitaire" offered intimate glimpses into the personal contributions and vulnerabilities of its members. "Into the Storm," in particular, stood as a bold affirmation of the band's capacity to rise above internal discord and external pressures, a melodic reminder that the journey of creation is as much about embracing the storm as it is about basking in the sunlight afterward.

In the end, "Fly From Here" is a story of contradictions—of nostalgia and innovation, of struggle and triumph. It is a narrative written in sound, a chapter in the long saga of Yes that speaks to both the weight of history and the promise of tomorrow. The album's creation was a testament to the band's willingness to confront its own legacy head-on—to delve into the storm of internal conflict and emerge with a sound that was unmistakably Yes, yet refreshingly new.

As the final notes of "Into the Storm" faded into silence, there was a palpable sense of closure—a moment when the echoes of the past and the whispers of the future converged. Yes had taken flight from the familiar confines of their legacy and soared into uncharted skies. In that act of defiant reinvention, they reaffirmed a simple truth: that even amidst the chaos of change, the human spirit—expressed through the universal language of music—remains indomitable.

Standing at the intersection of memory and ambition, the band members reflected on the journey that had led them to this point. They had weathered personal losses, navigated creative disagreements, and faced the daunting task of honoring a legacy while carving out a new path. Each instrument, each vocal line, was a testament to their shared history.

Today, as fans old and new continue to revisit "Fly From Here," they are reminded that the storm is not something to be feared but embraced. It is in the midst of turbulent winds that the beauty of flight is revealed—a beauty that lies not in the absence of conflict, but in the courage to navigate it. Yes's latest chapter is a vivid reminder that music, like life, is a journey defined by both the gentle breezes of hope and the fierce gales of change.

In this reflective moment, the album stands as a bridge—linking the raw energy of past epics with the modern pulse of contemporary rock. It is a chronicle of evolving identities, a narrative of reawakening, and ultimately, a celebration of the enduring magic that happens when a band refuses to be confined by its history. The storm, with all its dark clouds and brilliant flashes of light, becomes a canvas upon which the timeless art of Yes is painted.

And so, as the echoes of "Fly From Here" continue to resonate in quiet listening rooms and raucous concert halls alike, the story of Yes lives on. It is a story not just of music, but of human endeavor— a tale of how art can emerge from the most turbulent moments to reveal a sky full of possibilities. In every chord, every delicate pause, and every soaring refrain, there is a message: that even when the winds are at their fiercest, there is always a way to fly, to transcend, and to find new skies waiting beyond the storm.

Ultimately, "Fly From Here" is a declaration—a vivid statement that the creative journey is never truly over. It is an open invitation to listen, to reflect, and to soar alongside a band that has, time and again, proven that the essence of their art is rooted in the eternal quest for reinvention. In the quiet after the storm, Yes's music remains a beacon—a call to all who dare to dream, to struggle, and to fly from here into the boundless expanse of what lies ahead.

CHAPTER 03
HEAVEN & EARTH –
ESTABLISHING THE NEW
NORMAL

A hush settled over the studio lights, and a single beam caught the glimmer of anticipation in Chris Squire's eyes. He had stood on countless stages, recorded on legendary albums—but this was different. Standing beside him, Jon Davison gently cleared his throat. It was his first major studio release with Yes, a place Jon Anderson had held for decades. For loyal fans and curious newcomers alike, this moment felt like crossing a threshold into unexplored territory. It was the dawn of a new era.

On a breezy summer afternoon in 2014, the band convened in a Los Angeles rehearsal room to finalize the tracks for their twenty-first album. Outside, palm trees swayed, and the bright sun kissed the pavement with unwavering heat. Inside, the air was charged with both promise and anxiety, as if the walls were breathing in time with the band's heartbeat.

The task was both sacred and perilous. Jon Davison, stepping into a lineage of voices that shaped a genre, did not flinch. He arrived not to impersonate, but to extend the spirit. His voice, ethereal and high, shimmered with a familiar glow. It was easy to see why comparisons to Anderson emerged almost instantly. But there was something gentler, more grounded in his delivery—a humility that set him apart.

The opening track, "Believe Again," emerged like the first light of dawn—soft, promising, but not without its shadows. Co-written by Davison and Steve Howe, the song began the album in warm mid-tempo, driven by airy optimism and spiritual lyrics. Davison's tone was breezy and assured, intertwining with Squire and Howe's harmonies like old friends catching up after time apart. The production, however, muted the fire beneath the surface. Roy Thomas Baker's gloss polished away the grit. Alan White's drumming—usually the heartbeat of Yes— felt subdued, like a once-vibrant flame dimmed behind foggy glass. Even Howe later lamented that the wrong guitar takes made the final cut. Still, "Believe Again" planted a flag: this was not the Yes of *Relayer* or *Fragile*—but it was Yes, striving.

From the album's title to its sonic restraint, *Heaven & Earth* whispered of contrasts—between legacy and evolution, between skyward dreams and earthly limitations. The tracks that followed revealed a band leaning gently into change, careful not to fracture what remained sacred.

"The Game" followed, pulsing with a slightly stronger heartbeat. Penned by Davison and Squire—with contributions from longtime Squire collaborator Gerard Johnson—the track was one of the bassist's final gifts before his passing. It bore his fingerprints, even if they were too faint in the mix. The song opened with Howe's E-Bow guitar gliding like vapor over Downes' shimmering synths. The vocal was direct, confident. Squire's harmonies wrapped around the chorus like an embrace. Yet again, the production felt tentative. The drums lacked vitality; the bass, once a thunderous undercurrent, whispered from a distance. The track hinted at greatness, but never quite seized it. Still, on the 2014 tour, "The Game" blossomed into something stronger— proof that these new seeds needed time and stage-light to grow.

"Step Beyond" shifted tone, stepping through retro gates into a sonic past that was less '70s mysticism and more '80s neon. Programmed synthesizers dominated, cold and isolating. Davison's lyrics reached upward—hopeful, brave—but the arrangement fell short of their ambition. There were flickers of the old fire: Squire's bassline danced with nostalgic treble, and Howe's fretwork gleamed with finesse. But the track remained a curious interlude, more pop experiment than progressive voyage. The spirit was willing; the energy, restrained.

The inner dynamics of the band were evolving. Steve Howe, the sage figure, yearned for tighter arrangements. Chris Squire—always the soul of the rhythm—seemed both present and fading. Alan White, stalwart drummer of decades, fought to find space in these softer terrains. And Jon Davison, quietly determined, became not just a vocalist, but a songwriter shaping the new Yes from within.

"To Ascend," his collaboration with White, offered a moment of acoustic grace. Gentle and melancholic, the track embodied what *Heaven & Earth* so often tried to be: reflective, melodic, spiritual.

Davison's voice floated over Howe's pristine Portuguese guitar, with Downes' piano whispering beneath. But again, the production clipped the wings. White's drumming—thoughtful in spirit—lacked nuance in execution. The song felt almost there, like a painting left unfinished at the edges. A stripped-down acoustic version, released only in Japan, proved that beneath the polish, a purer truth was waiting.

"Light of the Ages," the only track solely written by Davison, marked a spiritual peak. Here, his lyrical voice found full form. The song explored Yes's classic motifs—light, transformation, cosmic seeking—with sincerity. Howe's steel guitar rippled like sunlight on water. White, for once, delivered a drum track that breathed, lifted. The coda surged with Davison's acoustic guitar and a rare blast from Squire's bass, as if the band was remembering how to fly. It was a glimpse—a promise of what this version of Yes could become.

"In a World of Our Own," born from Davison's Arizona visit with Squire, brought them closer both musically and emotionally. The song leaned into relationship themes, a personal narrative among the cosmic arcs. Squire's bass came forward, mingling with Downes' honky-tonk piano and synthesized vibraphone, while Davison lowered his register in a grounded, earnest vocal. Howe's Stratocaster added spice. But while pleasant, the song lacked the progressive bite to elevate it beyond "solid." Like much of the album, it existed in the middle distance—warm, familiar, but never transcendent.

Then came "It Was All We Knew." A Steve Howe solo effort that felt more like a footnote than a full statement. With a melody echoing past glories, the track looked inward, narrating a personal reflection on love and time. Davison gave it a journeyman vocal, doing what he could. But the production—flat, uninspired—offered little momentum. The breakdown held no spark. It was a song adrift, best suited for Howe's solo archive rather than this collective endeavor. A missed opportunity.

The final track, "Subway Walls," stood like a monument at the edge of the album's softer terrain. Co-written by Davison and Downes, it was the most overtly progressive moment on *Heaven & Earth*. The song opened with labyrinthine keyboards, shifting rhythms, and a sense of space that invoked *Close to the Edge*. Lyrically, it wandered through urban metaphors and existential questions. The imagery of subway walls, stained and worn, mirrored the band itself: aged, scarred, yet still carrying meaning. Squire's bass finally thundered. White's drums rose to meet the moment. And Davison soared—not in imitation, but in presence. It was a track that gestured toward what the whole album might have been with more time, more fire, more risk. And fittingly, it was the last studio work Squire would leave behind— a final bassline from the man who anchored Yes from the very beginning.

In fan forums and comment threads, emotions ran raw. Anderson's absence was an open wound. For many, *Heaven & Earth* was too soft, too cautious—a retreat from the bold, bewildering heights that made Yes legendary. Others found in Davison a kind of balm: a respectful steward, not a usurper.

Time, however, softened judgments. Repeated listens revealed quiet virtues. Listeners began to hear the album on its own terms— not as a successor to *Going for the One* or *Tales*, but as a vulnerable offering from a band trying not to disappear. The songs began to bloom in the memory like pressed flowers—delicate, imperfect, but lovingly placed.

In retrospect, *Heaven & Earth* may never be remembered as Yes's crowning achievement. But that was never its aim. It was a bridge, not a pinnacle—a necessary breath after a long climb. The album asked for patience, not applause. It offered continuity in place of revelation. And in doing so, it cleared the soil for whatever came next.

For Jon Davison, it was the beginning of authorship. For Chris Squire, it was the end of a luminous, irreplaceable journey. And for Yes, it was the moment they learned to walk again—not to run, not to ascend—but simply to believe again.

In a world where change is often feared, *Heaven & Earth* dared to be tender. It chose melody over majesty, reverence over reinvention. And in that quiet defiance, it kept the heart of Yes beating—however softly—for one more song, one more chapter, one more light in the dark.

CHAPTER 04
FROM A PAGE – REFLECTING ON LEGACY

A solitary beam of studio light slants across a cluttered mixing desk, dust motes floating like lost memories through its warm glow. The room hums quietly, filled with the distant echoes of unfinished music. This space, in Phoenix, Arizona, saw the birth—and shelving—of an album destined to linger, silent and unheard, for nearly a decade. "From a Page" began as whispers among Yes fans, elusive as morning mist, stirring a collective yearning for the unreleased and unknown.

Oliver Wakeman sits alone at the piano, fingers tracing the keys gently, like an archaeologist brushing dirt from ancient artifacts. Each note resurrects forgotten melodies, emotional relics left behind in the band's pursuit of grander visions. The album that became "Fly from Here" was meant to bear these creations, but a shift in the creative winds—with Trevor Horn at the helm—swept away Wakeman's compositions, replacing subtle introspection with sprawling ambition.

Fans, forever curious, speculated about these missing pieces. They envisioned what had been lost, glimpsing a version of Yes suspended between eras—between past brilliance and uncertain futures. The arrival of "From a Page" was not merely a musical release; it was the opening of a hidden chapter, pages gently turning to reveal emotional truths long obscured.

As listeners placed the needle upon vinyl, anticipation rippled outward. "To the Moment" bursts forth with Steve Howe's electric guitar, sharp and vibrant, set against the lush embrace of Wakeman's swirling keyboards. It felt like morning breaking after a storm, hopeful and radiant. Benoît David's voice emerged confident, neither shadowed by predecessors nor burdened by expectation. His vocal lines danced with Howe's acoustic threads, weaving through Alan White's rhythmic backbone and Chris Squire's robust bass—a poignant reminder of the bassist's irreplaceable presence. It was more than music; it was a spirited assertion of identity amidst change.

"Words On a Page" followed softly, an acoustic painting unfolding gently beneath David's contemplative vocal. Wakeman's piano lines shimmered like starlight across a tranquil lake, reflective and mesmerizing. Howe's slide guitar cut gently across the melody, evoking bittersweet nostalgia—a reminder of Yes's vintage roots. The lyrics spoke plainly yet poetically, evoking journeys into imaginative realms—magical worlds reachable only through music's profound alchemy.

But creative passions sometimes ignite internal storms. Beneath "From a Page," the careful listener can sense subtle fractures—the artistic tensions that led to these tracks' initial exclusion. Wakeman's compositions, meticulously produced and beautifully articulated, subtly clashed with the band's evolving creative trajectory under Horn. These unreleased songs whispered truths about Yes: the band's pursuit of excellence, their struggle with creative compromise, their determination to keep moving, even when the path was obscured.

Yet, in revisiting these lost pieces, healing emerged. The album's release after Chris Squire's passing transformed it into more than archival curiosity—it became an act of reverence. Wakeman, driven by the emotional weight of honoring Squire, ensured this material finally saw daylight, breathing closure and continuity into the band's legacy. Alan White embraced the project's resurrection, a symbolic gesture affirming Yes's enduring commitment to honoring every creative endeavor.

"From the Turn of a Card" emerges next—a stripped-down, intimate duet between Wakeman's expressive piano and David's earnest voice. It evokes the vulnerability of a midnight confession, delicate and uncertain, reflective of the band's own crossroads. The lyrics speak of fate's gentle uncertainty, choices laid bare, moments suspended precariously between past and future.

The mini-album concludes with "The Gift of Love," an expansive, collaborative piece involving every band member. Opening with Wakeman's majestic keys and Squire's signature bass, it rises and falls like a coastal tide—soothing yet powerful. David's vocals ring with sincerity, supported by Squire and Howe's harmonious backdrop. Though touched by musical fragments later echoed in "The Game," here the melody achieves a richer depth, culminating in an emotional crescendo. It ascends triumphantly, affirming love's transcendent power—a fitting finale marking Chris Squire's last studio footprint with Yes.

Fans received "From a Page" like rediscovering cherished photographs. Some embraced it as a hidden gem illuminating a lost era, others as a poignant memorial for Squire, still others felt an ambiguous nostalgia. But all experienced it as a bridge—a conduit between what Yes had been and what it was becoming. It was both a window and a mirror, prompting reflection on the band's legacy, their artistry, and the endless evolution of creative life.

Ultimately, "From a Page" stands as a reclaimed legacy—a vital fragment completing Yes's expansive narrative. Its existence reminds listeners that creativity transcends individual moments, enduring even through quiet obscurity. Like a treasured painting finally unveiled, the album enriches our understanding of Yes, underscoring the intricate beauty hidden within every stage of their journey.

The studio light fades gently, leaving only the soft hum of silence—an echo of music, now immortalized. In this quiet space, where memory and melody intertwine, the legacy of "From a Page" lingers, profound and enduring—a testament to the delicate art of preserving and honoring every note played and every story told.

CHAPTER 05
THE QUEST – PIONEERING A NEW IDENTITY

It's October 1, 2021. The air outside is crisp, the smell of change hanging thick as autumn leaves. Inside, a familiar sound swells, but it's not quite the same. Yes, the band that has held the heart of progressive rock for over five decades, now steps into uncharted waters with their album *The Quest*. No longer just continuing without Anderson, they are forging ahead—bold, unapologetic, and distinct. The absence of their founding member, Jon Anderson, is felt, but it's not a void. Instead, it's an invitation—an opportunity to create something new, a new sound that is still unmistakably Yes.

The album's title, *The Quest*, is more than just a name; it's a declaration. It's a statement of adventure, a metaphor for the unceasing exploration that defines Yes. With every chord, every note, they are venturing into unknown territories, pushing boundaries while respecting the legacy that shaped them. It's a call to arms for anyone who has ever felt the thrill of discovery, the pull of the unknown, and the belief that growth is born from challenge.

The band's newest members—Geoff Downes, Billy Sherwood, and Jon Davison—bring fresh perspectives to a legacy as entrenched as the band's. Yes is more than a band. Yes is a living, breathing force, evolving with every generation. The Quest is more than just an album; it's a declaration of that evolution.

In the shimmering light of *The Quest*, the boundaries of the past and the future dissolve like mist over a river at dawn. Classic Yes trademarks—lush harmonies, intricate musicianship, and the pioneering use of time signatures—are fused seamlessly with modern production techniques. *The Quest* is not a nostalgic rehash of what came before; it is the sound of the band re-imagining themselves. It's about innovation, yes, but also renewal. It's a leap forward, made with the same spirit that propelled them through decades of musical firsts.

Steve Howe, the constant through it all, has taken the reins with careful precision. His presence as both a producer and a guitarist reflects a balancing act between honoring the past and shaping the future. Tracks like "The Ice Bridge" epitomize this balance, blending classic symphonic arrangements with electronic synths, while songs like "Minus the Man" bring in progressive rock's familiar grandeur, but with a futuristic twist. The album's thematic core explores contemporary issues—climate change, artificial intelligence—subjects that root Yes's ethereal, otherworldly sounds in the pulse of today's world.

Despite being propelled by a new spirit of confidence, the band does not disregard their history. Howe's veteran status ensures that the soul of Yes remains intact, even as they test new musical waters. The Quest stands as a crossroads between tradition and innovation. The blending of orchestral touches with modern, edgy synths gives the album a unique feel, at once timeless and timely.

Steve Howe, as the unshakeable pillar of the band, is the architect. His guitar is the voice that leads the listener through *The Quest*. But this album is as much about the interplay of the old guard with the newcomers as it is about Howe's vision. Billy Sherwood, in his first full-time role as the bassist, doesn't simply fill the shoes left behind by Chris Squire; he shapes a new identity. Sherwood, a veteran in his own right, channels the spirit of his late mentor while infusing his own style, bringing energy that elevates the band's creativity.

Geoff Downes, the keyboardist who was underutilized in previous albums, finds ample space to experiment and showcase his artistry. His work here—particularly the ominous, evocative synth lines in "The Ice Bridge"—is some of his finest with Yes. Jon Davison's vocals, which had initially been questioned when he replaced Anderson, now soar with newfound depth. He's not just a replacement, but a collaborator, adding layers of emotion and lyrical storytelling. Davison's voice becomes a vessel for both the band's musical vision and the global concerns that shape the lyrics.

Each band member has a distinct role in the new chemistry of Yes. The collaborative synergy feels tangible, as though the band has found a new sense of purpose. This is a collective work, not just an aggregation of individual talent. The Quest is a testament to the power of collaboration, to the idea that an evolving band can be more than the sum of its parts.

Much like an epic novel, the tracks of *The Quest* unfold like chapters in a larger story. Each piece carries a sense of progression, moving from the introductory strains of "The Ice Bridge" to the sweeping musical landscapes of "A Living Island." The individual sections of each song are like mini-symphonies—each one tells a distinct part of the story while maintaining an overarching theme. "The Ice Bridge," for instance, is divided into three segments—"Eyes East," "Race Against Time," and "Interaction"—each one echoing a different aspect of the album's central theme of environmental crisis, hope, and connection.

The tracks are a journey themselves—musically, thematically, emotionally. From the breathtaking guitar solos of Howe in "Dare to Know" to the haunting string arrangements in "Leave Well Alone," the album traverses a range of sonic terrains. Howe's guitar weaves through the textures, both as a lead instrument and as a layering tool, creating moments of intricate beauty and intense, rich texture. The use of dynamic shifts—between the delicate piano parts of Geoff Downes and the thunderous drums of Alan White—creates a vast emotional landscape, reflecting the album's themes of discovery and renewal.

The bold songwriting choices do not simply stop at the arrangement of notes. They're about telling a story—about evoking feelings, thoughts, and memories. Yes's music, once considered an enigma by many, is now more accessible, even as it retains its progressive roots. They've bridged the gap between complexity and accessibility, with "The Ice Bridge" standing as an example of that delicate balance.

The album's reception has been a patchwork of cautious optimism and triumphant praise. Many critics hailed *The Quest* as a return to form. Some saw it as the band's ultimate redemption from the stagnation of their last album, *Heaven and Earth*. "The Ice Bridge," considered the standout track, was lauded as one of the band's finest moments in decades. The response was a recognition that, despite the loss of two founding members, Yes had not just survived; they had thrived.

But with every triumph comes resistance. Some detractors were quick to note that the album lacked the vitality of Yes's early work. The mellow tones, the lush arrangements, the introspective lyrics—all felt, to some, like a step backward. For them, *The Quest* could never live up to the heady days of *Fragile* or *Close to the Edge*. For others, though, this album was proof that Yes could still evolve, that the band's legacy was not confined to one era, one sound, or one group of musicians. They were, as ever, a band in flux—perpetually exploring, always expanding.

The Quest is a bold declaration of Yes's resilience. It is a moment where they embrace the future without losing the soul of their past. The album is a brave step forward, a new chapter in a saga that has spanned more than fifty years. It is not a nostalgic return to the past, but an evolution—one that will continue to unfold in the years to come. Yes has not just carried on without Anderson and Squire. They've built something new. In *The Quest*, they've found a new identity. They've proved that, even in a world that changes, some things remain eternal.

Yes's music, much like the quest itself, is never truly finished. The journey continues, as does the quest for discovery, reinvention, and the joy of creation. *The Quest* stands as a symbol not only of the band's longevity but of their capacity to continually reimagine their sound, their identity, and their legacy. In doing so, they've reaffirmed that Yes is not just a band, but an ongoing adventure.

CHAPTER 06
MIRROR TO THE SKY: PIONEERING A NEW IDENTITY

In the long dusk of rock's golden age, when many of its titans have either vanished or calcified into memory, *Mirror to the Sky* rises not like a monument but like a river returning to its source—restless, lyrical, eternal. It is not a comeback, nor a survival record. It is something braver: a reinvention born not of urgency but of acceptance. The Yes that made this album is no longer beholden to its past but has instead braided it into the present like a melody reprised in new key. In this story, music is not only art—it is lineage, a living entity threading the generations.

Jon Anderson's voice, once the lighthouse around which the band circled, is not here. But his spirit is not absent. Rather, it drifts through the album like mist on a meadow, touching certain phrasings, certain harmonic intervals, with a wistful kind of familiarity. The saga of Yes without him is not a tale of replacement, but of recalibration—a river flowing past a fallen stone, still urgent, still clear.

Mirror to the Sky, the third and finest movement in a trilogy that began with *Heaven & Earth*, is not a resurrection. It is a culmination— a chrysalis cracked not by nostalgia but by heat and pressure and a yearning to become more. The album unfolds like a novel written in symphonic language, each track a chapter not just in sound but in feeling, where orchestration replaces exposition and modulation becomes metaphor. It is, in every sense, a story sung into being.

Cut From the Stars — The return of the pulse. The album opens as if it has always been breathing, as if it merely waited for someone to press *play* and let the current through. "Cut From the Stars" strikes like desert lightning—no preamble, no easing in. Billy Sherwood's bass lunges forward, sinewed and muscular, less an instrument than a declaration. Its bite is matched by Steve Howe's twin guitars: one snarls, one shimmers. A Stratocaster growl in one channel, harmonic bells in the other. They don't argue—they dance like wind around stone.

Jay Schellen does not play drums here; he speaks with them, punctuating the air with odd-time urgency and then smoothing it into groove. Geoff Downes lets Hammond organ and Moog synths converse behind the vocal lines, not drawing attention to themselves but enlarging the song's breath. And Jon Davison sings as if standing barefoot in the desert, palms open to the stars. His voice is not Anderson's echo—it is its own moonlight. He sings of distance and cosmic kinship, of being made from celestial dust, and the song pulses forward like something remembered from a dream.

All Connected —Nine minutes and two seconds become both mirror and map. "All Connected" is a long, slow climb into the place where form and meaning fuse. Its three movements feel less like sections than perspectives, each building upon the last like sediment layers under a riverbed. Howe, Sherwood, and Davison co-compose not as individuals with parts, but as a single organism with multiple hearts.

The chorus lifts like a kite caught in thermal wind—"We are all connected / Nothing stands alone"—but it is no cheap platitude. It is a whispered truth delivered in a thunderstorm. Sherwood's backing vocals wrap Davison's like vines on trellis, creating a two-pronged harmony that evokes Yes's past with Trevor Rabin, yet feels firmly rooted in the now.

Downes weaves Mellotron echoes and organ sonorities beneath it all, while Schellen builds from feather-touch cymbal taps to cannon-fire toms, never forcing the transition, always inviting it. The result is hypnotic, like watching a city wake from above.

Luminosity — A Garden Grown from Grief. This song is sunlight pressed into sound. There is a gentleness in "Luminosity" that feels earned, not given—a serenity found only after walking through sorrow. Autoharp, mandolin, and banjo create a folk-laced bed of light, glimmering like dew on the edge of dawn. Sherwood's bass plays not to dominate but to lift, and Downes finds magic in celeste sparkle and synth flicker.

Davison sings of life as a "string of light we bend," and the line lands like a prayer—simple, true, luminous. The orchestral swell that closes the piece, written by Paul K. Joyce, doesn't rise so much as bloom, turning lyric into landscape. If *Heaven & Earth* was the exhale after heartbreak, *Luminosity* is the inhale before joy.

Living Out Their Dream — The Smile Behind the Curtain. This is the sly smile of the album, its tongue-in-cheek moment that plays like a carnival waltz. Don't be fooled by its short runtime—"Living Out Their Dream" is dense with wit and groove. Howe's ES-175 comping sits like a tuxedoed elder sipping scotch, while his Strat jabs like a mischievous cousin at a wedding. Downes leans into his Asia roots here, all bright synth stabs and playful Hammond punches.

Lyrically, the track pokes at ambition's mirage: the hunger for glory that devours joy. But it never scolds. It chuckles. Davison and Howe share vocals, their timbres playfully mismatched but woven like threads of different color. In a lesser band, this would be filler. In Yes, it is a winking interlude—a breath before the plunge.

Mirror to the Sky — The Cathedral Built from Echo. This is the keystone, the frescoed dome, the long reflection that gives the album its soul. Fourteen minutes of orchestral rock that neither shouts nor stumbles. It begins with a unison riff like an ancient bell tolling across canyons, and from there, it arcs into symphonic meditation. There are no wasted notes here. Each motif reappears in altered form, like themes in a novel returning with new meaning.

The center swells and then stills—nine minutes in, an acoustic hush falls like first snow. Howe's nylon-string whispers beside Downes's pastoral keyboards, and Sherwood's bass murmurs like a memory from childhood. Then, the build begins again. By the time the final refrain arrives—"Hold the mirror to the sky, see the dream that never dies"—we believe it, not as promise, but as evidence.

"Circle of Time" — The Fade and the Flame. The main album closes not with thunder but with twilight. "Circle of Time" is a quiet conversation with the soul. Howe's steel guitar sighs in wide, slow arcs, and Davison's voice floats above acoustic arpeggios like mist over a lake. The lyric contemplates time as neither enemy nor savior but companion—an echo walking beside us.

Joyce's strings do not swell here; they shimmer. A violin phrases a farewell not in sorrow, but in grace. This is the soft landing after a long flight, the moment when the journey becomes memory.

The bonus tracks are not add-ons—they are epilogues. "Unknown Place" surges with urgency, Stratocaster and Spanish guitar fencing in joyous combat. "One Second Is Enough" plays like a Zen koan made into rock song, short lines blooming into huge choruses. And "Magic Potion" is pure fun—Sherwood thumping, Downes dancing, Howe unspooling steel-guitar solos like ribbon through sky.

These songs show the band's playfulness, its refusal to let precision stifle curiosity. Even where Howe's voice strains, his intent sings louder: keep playing, keep dreaming.

The River Continues. Yes today is not Yes of 1971, nor of 1983, nor even 2011. It is a new constellation made from old stars, still orbiting a gravitational pull no single member defines. The departure of Anderson did not drain the river; it altered its course. Chris Squire's death deepened the current. Alan White's passing hollowed the bank. And yet, *Mirror to the Sky* does not feel like elegy. It feels like evolution.

The band's collaboration is scattershot in geography but united in intent—Zoom calls from Devon, stems sent from Seattle, bass lines emailed from Los Angeles. They are no longer a rock band in the touring-bus sense. They are a collective, a living manuscript written in six decades of harmonics and heartache.

At concerts, teenagers sway beside retirees, both mouthing the same lyrics. That, perhaps, is the truest legacy: a music not trapped in time, but traveling through it, forever shifting its light.

Like the river it resembles, *Mirror to the Sky* is not done. It loops back on itself, reflecting sun and storm alike. It sings of loss not as ending, but as opening. In it, Yes does not merely survive—it glows.

CHAPTER 07
PHOTOGRAPHS – YES IN CONCERT

(All photographs in this chapter were taken by me, the author.)

Billy Sherwood - Yes in Baltimore, MD 2015

Yes at Atlanta Symphony Hall 2.14.17 (Billy Sherwood)

The late Alan White of Yes - 8/7/17 Baltimore, MD

Billy Sherwood of Yes - 8/7/17 Baltimore, MD

Jon Davison and Steve Howe of Yes - 8/7/17 Baltimore, MD

Steve Howe of Yes - 8/7/17 Baltimore, MD

Me with Yes - 8/7/17 Baltimore, MD

Yes In Atlanta GA 7/28/2018 - Steve How and Geoff Downes

Yes, Nashville, TN

Steve Howe of Yes- Atlanta GA

Jon Davison / Yes in Baltimore, MD 2015

Steve Howe and Jon Davison

Steve Howe- Yes in Baltimore, MD 2015

Geoff Downes - Yes in Baltimore, MD 2015

Billy Sherwood - Yes in Baltimore, MD 2015

Geoff Downes of Yes at Atlanta Symphony Hall 2.14.17

CHAPTER 08
TWIDDLEY BITS

It begins like a whisper from a dream, half-remembered but sharply felt—a breath of air in the cathedral of sound. Somewhere beneath the grandeur of towering symphonic rock, beneath labyrinths of shifting time signatures and ascending arpeggios, lies a thread so fine it's almost invisible: the Twiddley Bits. Rick Wakeman once named it with a wry grin—"the little Twiddley Bits I add so nobody gets bored"—and ever since, that playful phrase has hummed like a secret password among the initiated. It sounds like mischief, like levity. But inside Yes, it is scripture.

To hear a Twiddley Bits is to feel the architecture of a song breathe. It is sunlight glancing off stained glass, smoke curling in a still room: ornament and essence at once, the smallest gesture whispering the band's largest truths. With Yes, virtuosity is not a boast; it is a language, and the Twiddley Bits is its comma, its exclamation, its sly aside.

Every language, however, must survive its storms. The tempest that bore *Union* was not thunder but ink—paper contracts, broken phone lines, and the tired drag of ego. In the faltering dusk of 1991, the world's greatest progressive-rock band found itself cleaved in two—Squire and Rabin's modern Yes West on one side, Anderson Bruford Wakeman Howe's venerable quartet on the other—and sewn together again by managerial decree. Two bloodstreams now pulsed inside one stitched skin, unsure which heartbeat was truly their own.

Yet even under fluorescent board-room light the Twiddley Bits refused to wilt; they sprouted like green shoots pushing through asphalt. On the very first breath of the album, a mechanized heartbeat rises into focus, and suddenly *Lift Me Up* lurches into being. Trevor Rabin's guitar, clean and angular, arcs above Alan White's drum program like scaffolding in a neon skyline, while Chris Squire coils his bass in double-helix motifs that wink back toward *Fragile*. The song's bones are radio-ready, polished for airplay, but a flash of Wakeman's staccato synth—just a ladder of lightning after each chorus—opens a skylight in the glossy ceiling, reminding anyone who listens closely that this band will never be simplified.

The atmosphere shifts, reggae dusts the rhythm, and *Saving My Heart* ambles into view. Rabin sings here with suave fatigue, Anderson joining him like a shaft of sunlight tracing the edge of a skyscraper. Beneath their harmonies, White's snare snaps and Squire's bass slips a counter-melody, nervous and tender, until midway through the track Steve Howe releases a sixteen-note slide-guitar pirouette. The phrase whirls above the mix for only a breath—a firefly over city traffic—but its glow says: *I am still here. I still remember.*

Promise swells when *Miracle of Life* unfurls: synth pads shimmer like a crane shot gliding over Los Angeles at twilight, acoustic guitars flicker like boulevards lit by halogen. Squire's fretless loops circle restlessly, Rabin's arpeggios flash like paparazzi bulbs. Yet cohesion slips away; Anderson arrives not as epiphany but adornment, and the track loops its refrain the way a film gets stuck in its projector gate. The parts sparkle; the glue falters. In progressive rock, even miracles can stall mid-flight.

Then the room stills for *Masquerade*. Howe, alone with an acoustic, records in a single take—fifteen minutes of unfiltered grace sharpened down to two and a half. Thumb-pops, harp rolls, glissando harmonics: Twiddley Bits that confide rather than boast, brushing across the listener's skin like a lover's breath. The Grammy nomination later pinned on its sleeve feels almost beside the point; in its hush the piece murmurs more truth than many full-length opuses dare.

Among the album's noise and neon, a quieter chamber opens when Squire and Billy Sherwood offer *The More We Live – Let Go*. Synthesizers spiral like thoughts before sleep, and two voices—one seasoned, one searching—fold together in gentle resolve. No fireworks, no sprawled virtuosity; instead the song settles across ruined ground like first snowfall, accepting what cannot be rebuilt and choosing peace instead.

The chronology rewinds, engines whir, and we land in 1982's transitional heat, where *Make It Easy* hums with architectural promise. Rabin, White, and Squire play like engineers laying bullet-train track: jazz-fusion sparks fly, harmonic steel glints, and then—blueprint rolled up—the song ends, nothing more than a whisper before the shout of "Owner of a Lonely Heart."

That shout arrives fully inked when *It Can Happen* spreads its wings. Rabin's electric sitar ripples across still water, Squire's bass leaps like a dolphin in tinted dusk, Anderson sings with crystalline calm, and the lyric—direct, unmasked—tells of pressure, consequence, choice. Progressive textures cradle pop bones, and the voices twine in credible conviction: *change is possible.*

Lyrically, "It Can Happen" doesn't touch the mysticism of Anderson's typical lyrics, but it does match the streamlined profile of Yes's music—and the album overall.

It's a constant fight
A constant fight
You're pushing the needle to the red,
Black, and white
Who knows who's right
No substitute you're born you're dead
Fly by night
Created out of fantasy
Our destinations call

The Cinema version, available on the deluxe reissue of 90125, shows Chris Squire and Trevor Rabin building a powerful track—and Squire's vocals are just as convincing as those that replaced him.

Vulnerability seldom surfaces in Yes, but it seeps through *Love Conquers All,* penned by Squire and Sherwood like a late-night confession on hotel stationery. Rabin sings with soft conviction, keyboards remain polite, production stays within tidy borders—yet in that restraint a rare mineral glints: the band not as cosmic pilgrims or technical titans, but as men who bleed.

We leap backward once more to 1983, where the broadcast anthem "Owner of a Lonely Heart" scorches its mark. Rabin's guitar dive-bomb at three-minutes-and-five lasts barely a measure, yet etches a Twiddley Bits into MTV's retina forever—proof that grandeur thrives on brevity when the fire is bright enough.

Digital dawn colors the horizon of 1997, and *New State of Mind* bursts open with Sherwood's studio sheen. Squire's bass is volcanic, White's drums punchy, Howe's sitar ghosts in like incense from an earlier age, and Anderson pierces the circuitry with soprano light. Optimism—manufactured, maybe, but earnest—crackles across the chorus, a renovation rather than a betrayal.

Open Your Eyes follows not as song but as manifesto. Porcaro's keyboards sparkle like city lights through rain, Howe's steel swoops in late—an old friend navigating a new-world party—while Sherwood's architecture holds the beams steady. Together Squire and Anderson climb not to heaven but to comprehension: open eyes, acknowledge both decay and dazzle, and keep building.

Sherwood's production pushed Alan White's drums and Chris Squire's bass front and center. Additionally, the vocal interplay between Jon Anderson and Squire was magical.

You've got a great imagination

You carry on in the same old way

No lessons learned from yesterday

Talk of changes lost in pages of paperwork

I believe it …

How can we refuse to see

I've received it…

What could be our final destiny

I believe that …

Still we go on from day to day

Knowing what could be true

Wish I knew

Wish I knew

Wish I knew

Sherwood has knack for melding traditional Yes elements with a contemporary sound. "Open Your Eyes" served as the first single from the album, and reached No. 33 on the mainstream rock charts.

Track by track they negotiate legacy. Even in *Universal Garden*, whose lush canopy Howe once dismissed, guitars braid above Anderson's eco-spiritual musings, Sherwood's synth horns and Squire's bass conjuring a biosphere of sound: Yes at its most entwined, vines rooted deep, leaves kissing starlight. Then *Man on the Moon* drifts in, playful and half-remembered, its nursery-rhyme lyric carving innocence into stone while tribal percussion rocks the song like an ancient cradle.

Closing time arrives, but *The Solution* refuses neat farewell. Melodies surge forward, retreat, surge again like a tide unsure of allegiance to shore or sea. Anderson begins with assurance, Sherwood's swirling synths wrap like mist, Squire and Howe lift the frame until, without warning, silence drops—or almost. A hidden ambient landscape unfolds, the band lingering in corridors of echo as though uncertain how to leave the room, as if sound itself were reluctant to rest.

All these songs—bold radio bids, fragile miniatures, experiments that breathe digital neon—populate the novel-length middle of our tale. They reveal a band forever negotiating between ambition and survival, between cosmic intent and corporate demand, between the child sketching stars in margins and the executive signing contracts downtown. Across every rift, the Twiddley Bits arc like lightning bridges, tiny yet electric, testifying that fingers still itch to color outside the lines.

The idea Wakeman once tossed off has evolved in the larger world: Dave Stewart's Twiddly Bits MIDI libraries now offer virtuoso flourishes as drag-and-drop code, turning handcrafted grace into downloadable asset. Evolution and eulogy share a single pulse; even compressed to integers, a Twiddley Bits carries the joy of unnecessary beauty, the reminder that precision plus irreverence equals flight.

Peers spoke this dialect too: Genesis slipping harpsichord trails through "Firth of Fifth," King Crimson's ice-pick guitar runs in "Larks' Tongues in Aspic," ELP flinging ragtime confetti across Moog cathedrals. Yet Yes built an entire lexicon: listen to Wakeman's Moog squiggle, Bruford's cymbal hiccup, Howe's harmonic chirp, Squire's descending stair of bass. It is dialogue, not soloing—jazz spoken with a British accent and Baroque vowels. On stage the ritual still blooms: Howe never paints "Siberian Khatru" the same twice, Wakeman scribbles fresh riffs mid-"Awaken," each Twiddley Bits a seed of resurrection.

Strip those bits away and the landscape flattens; humanity drains. For these flourishes are not indulgence; they are intimacy—the trill Bach tucks into a perfect fugue, Coltrane's half-second linger before the saxophone dives. They remind us that every architect secretly loves doodling suns in the corner of the blueprint.

So *Union* endures as paradox, stitched by commerce yet pulsing with wonder. In its cracks we find progressive rock's great wager: that complexity need not crush joy, that ambition can grin, that a single unnecessary grace-note can save an empire of sound. The Twiddley Bits, once a joke, has proved a fingerprint—proof that music, like life, refuses to be merely functional.

Lean closer. In *Close to the Edge* you'll hear an electric whisper skitter between thunderheads. In *Union* you'll see the sapling twirl through asphalt. Follow the path through remixes, bootlegs, reunions; note how every night Howe still winks a new harmonic, Wakeman cracks open another Moog surprise, Squire's spectral bass descends a staircase in your memory. Something always waits in the corner of the soundscape—a secret sparkle, a six-note flicker saying, *you are listening to something alive.*

And if you dare, answer. Add your own flourish, your own glint of unnecessary beauty. Because even a second can sing—and in that brief shimmer, the whole cathedral may breathe again.

CHAPTER 09
THE PRESENT STATE – "KIT AND CABOODLE"

The London dusk settled like a slow exhale. In the back room of a modest rehearsal space not far from where the band once laid its earliest tracks, Steve Howe stood quietly tuning his Gibson ES-175. The warm hum of tube amps, the idle clatter of cables, and the low murmur of technicians formed a subtle chorus behind him. A few feet away, Geoff Downes adjusted the levels on his keyboard rig, fingers fluttering over the digital display like a pianist practicing muscle memory. There was no ceremony, no thunderous cue that marked the beginning of a session—just the quiet rhythm of experienced hands at work. It was 2023, and Yes was still a band.

More accurately, Yes was still a working band—touring, recording, refining. The decades behind them, full of tectonic shifts in the music industry and within their own ranks, seemed less like burdens and more like milestones—weathered markers in a long, winding career. To understand the present state of Yes is to confront a rare story in modern music: one not driven by nostalgia or the mere recitation of past glories, but by an ongoing process of creative survival. Where other bands grew brittle with time, Yes absorbed change and turned it into continuity.

In its current incarnation, the band comprises five individuals whose collective resumes thread through nearly every era of Yes's evolving identity. Steve Howe, the guitarist whose nimble phrasing and textural sensitivity had helped define the band's sound since 1970, now carried the symbolic and functional role of elder statesman. At his side was Geoff Downes, the keyboardist whose entrance in 1980 during the Drama sessions had once been considered a disruption, now redefined as lineage. Billy Sherwood, a longtime associate and occasional member since the '90s, assumed the mantle of bassist in 2015 after the passing of founding member Chris Squire—an event that sent tremors through the core of Yes's history. Jon Davison, the lead vocalist since 2012, brought a spiritual and vocal continuity to Jon Anderson's high-register mystique, while Jay Schellen, the most recent addition in 2023, took up the drum throne after years of shadowing the late Alan White. Five musicians. One name. Dozens of lives folded into one.

The road to this present ensemble was never linear. If Yes's early years were marked by experimentation and excess—symphonic structures, fantastical themes, double-album ambitions—then its middle years were defined by commerce and compromise. The 1980s brought reinvention, the 1990s fragmentation, and the early 2000s a tenuous balance between legacy and forward motion. Lineup changes were frequent, sometimes acrimonious, other times strangely seamless. By 2023, the band had cycled through 20 full-time members, each contributing to an intricate mosaic of sound and sensibility. For some, the rotating door of personnel might suggest instability. But in the case of Yes, turnover became an unlikely engine of endurance.

To trace the band's lineage is to follow a near-geological layering of styles and philosophies. From Jon Anderson's lyrical metaphysics and Chris Squire's trebly, contrapuntal bass lines to Rick Wakeman's Baroque flourishes and Alan White's dependable backbeat, Yes evolved as much through its internal contrasts as through its shared goals. Steve Howe, long regarded as the connective tissue across many of these iterations, often cited "the sound of Yes" as a living organism—something larger than its parts, demanding of care but capable of adapting. That ethos would prove essential in the wake of loss.

Chris Squire's death in 2015 was more than a personal tragedy. It raised an existential question: could Yes continue without its only constant member? Squire had not only played on every album until then; he had been the band's compass, creatively and legally. His decision to pass the bass role to Billy Sherwood—his longtime friend, collaborator, and spiritual protégé—was both pragmatic and symbolic. In effect, he anointed continuity. The gesture wasn't about replacement, but trust. Sherwood stepped into the role not as a mimic but as a steward, preserving the rhythmic and harmonic character of Squire's work while weaving in his own compositional instincts.

Alan White's death in 2022, after years of declining health and intermittent absences from touring, presented a similar challenge. Yet even before his passing, Jay Schellen had become a quiet fixture in the band's live setup—learning the intricacies of White's playing not by rote, but through immersion. His eventual elevation to full-time member was less a disruption than a natural progression. With Howe guiding the musical direction and Downes anchoring the harmonic framework, the current configuration of Yes began to find its own cadence.

That cadence manifested most audibly in Mirror to the Sky, the band's 2023 release and their twenty-third studio album. Dedicated to White's memory, the record reached back into the band's progressive roots with long-form compositions, dynamic time signatures, and thematic cohesion. It was not a reinvention, but a reaffirmation. While critics noted echoes of Close to the Edge and Relayer, longtime fans recognized something more important: sincerity. Yes wasn't chasing their past. They were carrying it forward.

On stage, the band's presence remained distinctively measured— less about spectacle and more about precision. Recent tours across Europe, North America, and Japan drew crowds of varying generations, many of whom brought with them the quiet reverence of longtime listeners. Yes shows, by this point, resembled rituals more than concerts: multi-part suites played in full, subtle re-voicings of classic melodies, the occasional nod to deep cuts that only devoted fans would recognize. The band wasn't trying to prove anything. They were simply showing up—playing with intention, honoring the music, and, in the process, asserting their right to continue.

Their touring schedule remained demanding. In 2024 alone, Yes played a spring run across Europe, joined Deep Purple for a co-headlining U.S. tour in late summer, and then crossed the Pacific for dates in Japan. Plans for 2025 were already underway, including a North American tour and the beginnings of another studio album. Behind the scenes, Downes had begun programming new keyboard textures, and Sherwood had posted photos of recording sessions in Los Angeles, teasing a sound both exploratory and familiar. For a band deep into its sixth decade, this pace would be impressive. For Yes, it was simply another cycle in a continuum.

But why continue? Why persist when the original founders were largely gone, when the industry itself had fractured into streaming algorithms and retro playlists? The answer lies not in commerce or ego, but in the deeper architecture of purpose. Yes was never just a band; it was a proposition—musical, spiritual, even philosophical. Built on the belief that complexity could be beautiful and ambition wasn't antithetical to accessibility, Yes offered listeners a way to engage with music as journey rather than product. To retire that idea would mean conceding to a culture that increasingly prizes brevity over depth.

There was also, undeniably, a sense of duty. Steve Howe, now in his mid-70s, had spoken openly about legacy—not as something to be entombed in retrospectives, but as something to be lived. His stewardship of the band emphasized craftsmanship over charisma. He rarely gave interviews that veered into nostalgia, instead focusing on arrangements, performance quality, and audience engagement. Similarly, Jon Davison saw his role not as a stand-in for Jon Anderson but as a bridge—someone who could evoke the spirit of the music while contributing his own character. Their alignment was less about replication than resonance.

This sense of stewardship extended beyond the band's internal culture. In recent years, Yes had begun curating archival releases, remastering early albums, and collaborating with documentary filmmakers to preserve their history with clarity and accuracy. Far from resting on their past, they were organizing it—turning legacy into something generative. Fans responded in kind, not only attending shows but participating in discussions, forums, and retrospectives that treated the band's history with scholarly interest. The Yes community, once scattered and cultish, now operated like a living archive.

Still, questions lingered. Could Yes remain relevant in a world increasingly defined by speed and simplification? Would future generations find their way to the band's labyrinthine catalog, or would the music recede into the footnotes of progressive rock history? These questions were not unique to Yes. They haunted every legacy act still in motion, from King Crimson to Genesis, from Rush to The Who. Yet Yes seemed uniquely suited to answer them—not through declarations, but through action.

Their resilience wasn't loud. It didn't demand headlines or viral moments. Instead, it moved like water around stone—adapting, reshaping, persisting. They kept recording. They kept touring. They kept showing up. And in doing so, they demonstrated a kind of quiet defiance: the belief that music, when built with care and sustained with intention, could outlast the winds of trend and time.

As the session wound down that evening in London, Jay Schellen gave his snare one last tap and set the sticks across the toms. Geoff Downes powered down his synths, the lights dimming slightly as the power cycled. Steve Howe unplugged his guitar with a soft click and coiled his cable with practiced grace. No fanfare. No declarations. Just the quiet satisfaction of work done well—and the subtle anticipation of what would come next.

Because for Yes, there was always a next.

CHAPTER 10
LEGACY REFLECTIONS AND ROUNDTABLE

The damp breath of an autumn evening lay over North London, softening the amber glow of streetlamps and carrying faint echoes of traffic along the Holloway Road. Inside a low-slung brick rehearsal space—once a Victorian laundry, now re-purposed for music—the hush of anticipation preceded the day's final playback. Coil-bound lyric sheets rustled, instrument cases lined a wall like battered steamer trunks, and a single red standby lamp winked above a Studer tape machine. It was here, in this unassuming room, that a select gathering convened to look backward with purpose and, in doing so, trace the living arc of Yes.

Seated around a scarred oak table were Mark Anthony K—bandleader for Projekt Gemineye and co-host of the *Yes Music Podcast*—writer and lifelong devotee Preston Frazier, and a handful of technicians whose careers had intersected with the group's restless catalogue. They had come not to debate the canonical classics—*Fragile*, *Close to the Edge*—but to explore *Drama*, the 1980 release that at once fractured and reaffirmed the Yes identity. The ambience felt more colloquy than celebration; coffee steamed in enamel mugs while a quiet reel of memories unspooled.

Preston opened proceedings with the direct warmth of a fan who had learned to balance affection with analysis. "For years," he remarked, fingers drumming a gentle 5/4 against the tabletop, "I called this their guitarist's record. Howe's palette is extraordinary—Les Paul Junior for bite, ES-175 for breadth, steel and Tele for color. He's leaner, dirtier, yet never reckless." He cited the slugged-down descending figure that launches "Machine Messiah," noting how its saturated harmonic interplay with Geoff Downes's Prophet-5 creates a timbre almost orchestral in density. The others nodded; the point felt incontestable.

Mark leaned forward, voice low but animated. "That opening was Alan White's doing," he said, referencing an interview culled from

Tom Morse's exhaustive session diaries. "He arrived one morning with that stuttering 12/8 groove and insisted the rest of the band 'build a cathedral' upon it. Squire doubled the riff an octave lower on his Mouradian CS-74, Howe dialled the Marshall beyond its usual sweet spot, and suddenly the song breathed steam." He paused, letting the technical detail settle before adding, "It is progressive metal in embryo—years before the genre adopted the term."

All discussion of *Drama* inevitably curved toward personnel. With Jon Anderson and Rick Wakeman gone, many listeners had assumed the spirit of Yes would evaporate. Yet the enlistment of Trevor Horn and Geoff Downes, imported from The Buggles, injected not just new blood but a fresh technological mindset. Downes arrived armed with a Fairlight CMI—the first digital sampling workstation to reach mainstream recording—while Horn brought pop-producer meticulousness already evident in his pre-production notes. The pair were younger, schooled in synth-pop brevity, yet unafraid of odd-meter labyrinths.

Preston recalled early fan reactions: boos reported during the UK warm-up tour, open letters lamenting the absence of Anderson's alto. "The shift felt seismic," he admitted, "but it was also necessary. Bands that stagnate on sentimentality tend to ossify. *Drama* showed elasticity." Mark agreed, adding that the album's 38-minute runtime— short by Yes standards—demonstrated an editor's discipline without relinquishing compositional breadth. "Six tracks, no filler," he said. "Compact, yet panoramic."

A battered JBL monitor kicked on, and the engineer cued "Man in a White Car." The track's skeletal architecture—Fairlight stabs, marimba accents, and Trevor Horn's plaintive vocal—floated through the room. Mark pointed out the Fairlight's Page R sequencer data later printed inside the deluxe reissue booklet, lines of hexadecimal that had effectively become sheet music for the digital age. "It is chamber music recast in silicon," he observed. "The harmonic movement is simple, but the timbral envelope unfolds like brushed steel."

Talk turned to production. Eddie Offord, whose fingerprints graced *Fragile* and *Close to the Edge*, began the sessions but left after a series of unexplained absences—rumours ranged from burnout to creative disagreement. Hugh Padgham stepped in, wielding his trademark gated-reverb techniques later immortalised on *Invisible Touch* and *Synchronicity*. The difference is immediately audible: snares crack like shutter releases, kicks bloom then vanish, toms sound tuned rather than thumped. Preston compared it to "placing the drums in an anechoic chamber lit by fluorescents—every transient exposed, no shadow unresolved."

They listened next to "Does It Really Happen?". Here, Chris Squire's eight-string Ranney custom roared with a mid-range growl, strings doubled in octaves that created built-in chorus. No guitar solo surfaced; instead, Howe threaded motif after motif—short, contrapuntal cells that functioned less as showcase and more as structural glue. Mark called it "architectonic humility," the choice to forgo heroics in service of dynamic contour.

Over the tapes, Billy Sherwood's voice entered the conversation via pre-recorded interview. He spoke of meeting Squire in 1989, dissecting the *Drama* stems during late-night sessions. "Chris told me," the playback crackled, "that bass on 'Does It Really Happen?' was his attempt to marry Entwistle articulation with McCartney melody. He wanted front-house clarity without sacrificing bottom-end heft." When Squire's health began to falter decades later, Sherwood continued, the elder bassist handed him the white-finished Mouradian and said, simply, "Make it speak." The room fell silent, each attendee grasping the weight beneath those three words.

From Sherwood the discourse broadened to the idea of custodianship. Yes, the participants agreed, functioned less as a fixed ensemble and more as a modular organism. Jon Anderson once likened the band to a symphony in which chairs could change yet the score endured. Steve Howe, in a separate interview excerpt, described his role as "keeper of the fretboard vernacular," ensuring that signature counter-melodies remained audible even as keyboard tones shifted from Mini-Moog to Nord Stage.

Rick Wakeman's recorded comments provided counterbalance— equal parts humour and candour. He recalled arriving at Heathrow in 1979, cape stuffed into a garment bag, only to discover rehearsals had been cancelled. "Jon and I were effectively redundant," he laughed. "Yet to hear 'Machine Messiah' now is to recognise that the lads navigated without us just fine." Wakeman praised Downes for avoiding excessive ornamentation, crediting him with "precision where I might have added renaissance frills."

The engineer queued "Into the Lens," and the Fairlight's grainy sample of Downes's own voice—fed through an EMS Vocoder—rippled through the monitors. Trevor Horn endured nightly throat-strain to overlay Squire's towering harmonies, marking one of the few times a Yes track featured a lead vocal outside the Anderson register. Mark observed how the song's alternating 5/4 and 6/4 bars give it a subtle forward lurch, "like a documentary dolly shot that never quite centres."

Fan reception, once mixed, has mellowed into admiration. Streaming statistics presented by a quiet analyst in the corner revealed *Drama* now ranks fourth in the band's back-catalogue for monthly plays, narrowly behind *Fragile* and *Close to the Edge* but ahead of *Tormato* and *Going for the One*. Younger listeners cite its concise runtime and heavier textures as gateways into the labyrinthine world of seventies prog.

A brief intermission found the group examining Alan White's drum charts, photocopied from the original Morgan Studios ledger. Ghost-notes peppered the staves; odd groupings of seven and nine dotted eighths hinted at the drummer's fondness for nested polyrhythms. Mark traced a china-cymbal hit atop bar sixty-four of "Tempus Fugit" and smiled. "He placed that accent knowing it would never land on a downbeat. Displacement was his secret weapon."

Returning to playback, "Run Through the Light" revealed its unusual personnel swap: Trevor Horn on fretless Wal bass, Squire hammering clavinet through an MXR Phase 90. Howe's cherry-red Les Paul Junior cut through with razor articulation, a reminder that he could channel punk economy when required. The chorus floated in an almost-lyrical ambiguity—*Run through the light, run through forever*—inviting interpretation rather than prescribing meaning.

The evening's final spin belonged, inevitably, to "Tempus Fugit." The track, at 5:15, condensed all of *Drama's* trademarks—syncopated unison riffs, modal key shifts, call-and-response vocals—into a single, kinetic statement. Squire's eight-string lines, doused in flanger and stereo delay, ricocheted across the control room, and Howe's

Stratocaster filled the interstices with staccato jabs. "It is," Preston concluded, "Yes distilled to adrenaline."

With the musical autopsy complete, attention shifted to legacy. The group traced Yes's trajectory from London youth-club experiment to Rock & Roll Hall of Fame inductees. They spoke of the band's capacity for reinvention: Anderson Bruford Wakeman Howe's union with the Rabin-era line-up; the symphonic ventures of *Magnification*; the pastoral renaissance of *The Quest* and *Mirror to the Sky*. Each phase carried echoes of its predecessors yet answered contemporary climates—digital sampling in the eighties, orchestral integration in the zeros, modern mastering aesthetics today.

Billy Sherwood's recorded words returned for coda. "I view Yes as a relay," he said. "Chris passed me the bass baton. When my time ends, someone else will shoulder it. The melody remains." Jon Anderson, in a separate clip, likened their oeuvre to *the idea of flight— wing-beats sometimes falter, but lift returns.* Steve Howe, characteristically succinct, offered, "The guitar line goes on."

As reel one wound down and the Studer switched into standby, the room exhaled. Mark gathered his notes; Preston capped his fountain pen. Outside, the city's night pulse persisted, indifferent yet diminished behind double-glazing. Nothing decisive had been pronounced, yet something essential had been reaffirmed: *Drama* was not a footnote but a fulcrum, proof that identity can adapt without dissolving.

In the corridor, someone flicked off the fluorescent work-lights, leaving only the studio's green exit sign to cast long shadows over flight-cases. The group dispersed with quiet handshakes and promises to meet again—perhaps when the next chapter revealed itself in a set-list or a reissue's bonus disc. The chill air awaited them, but so did the comforting knowledge that the story of Yes, like its modulating time signatures, moved forward in continuous variation.

And so this chapter closes—not with a terminal cadence, but with a suspended harmony, a note held in collective memory until the next downbeat invites the song to rise once more.

1. Additional Interview: Yes bassist Billy Sherwood (2017)

Billy Sherwood joined Preston Frazier for an interview as Yes prepares to release *Topographic Drama: Live Across America*, a document of the band's full-album concert presentations of 1973's *Tales from Topographic Oceans* and 1980's *Drama*.

PRESTON FRAZIER: Billy, I first sat down with you two years ago. A lot has changed for you and Yes. For instance, *Topographic Drama: Live Across America* includes the entire concert, encores and all, pulled from 12 different shows. Why the change in the format this time around?

BILLY SHERWOOD: I had a hard drive filled with all the shows. I sifted through a bunch to find the best performances of each song, and decided why not use the best of the best? There are no rules that say one has to use only one particular show. As you mentioned, this is a different approach than *Like It Is*. It's even done differently than from the previous live Yes DVD and CDs. *Live Across America* is different in that way, and becomes unique in its creation.

PRESTON FRAZIER: I had the opportunity to see you guys in Chicago – where we met in the parking lot – and right after the Cruise to the Edge in Atlanta. Both shows were incredibly tight. Jay Schellen sat in on both shows. As that tour progressed, how did it change? Is Alan White included on this recording?

BILLY SHERWOOD: The record is a mixture of Alan and Jay. They play so much alike, the consistency of the drums is such that by the time I was done I had no idea who played what. I know I played bass and sang! [Laughs.]

PRESTON FRAZIER: What was the most challenging moment for you?

BILLY SHERWOOD: "Ritual". It's a very intensely bass-driven song, and there is also a bass solo within it. My challenge was to retain the notes and emotional content which Chris Squire brought to it while finding my own thing inside it, as well. To that end, I tried my best to remain true to the iconic bass moments that we all know and love, and then expand on it and bring my own dimension to it. I think it worked quite well and represents both Chris and myself in a very nice way. As a Yes fan, it was something important to me to do. "Ritual" is one of my favorite pieces on *Tales*, and there is a special honor that comes with playing it in Yes. As this is the first-ever Yes record to be released without Chris Squire on it, I took extra care to try to make it the best it could be.

PRESTON FRAZIER: You mixed the *Like It Is* series of live albums. Did you reprise that role for *Topographic Drama: Live Across America?*

BILLY SHERWOOD: I mixed the record. The band trusted I knew the Yes sound.

PRESTON FRAZIER: Now that you are a member of the band, did that role create any tension or difficulty?

BILLY SHERWOOD: Safe to say after all these years working with the band, touring, producing, playing etc., I knew the vibe well. *Tales* is my favorite Yes record, and so my instincts to make it feel like the original – sonically speaking – came easy. Long story short, the band trusts in me to get that Yes sound.

PRESTON FRAZIER: On your tour diary for the YEStival tour, there is a segment where you are recording Yes singer Jon Davison with a remote recording unit. Were those recordings for a new project, or overdubs for *Topographic Drama?*

BILLY SHERWOOD: Jon and I were working on an entirely different project in that diary clip you mentioned, nothing to do with Yes.

PRESTON FRAZIER: Were any parts of *Topographic Drama: Live Across America* overdubbed?

BILLY SHERWOOD: No, there were no overdubs. This is why I choose the best overall takes to compile the record. Each track was played and sang as you hear it. All I did was mix it.

PRESTON FRAZIER: Yes seems to have big plans for 2018. What else can you disclose?

BILLY SHERWOOD: Just a great year celebrating 50 years of my all-time favorite band – a band that somehow fate guided me to and set me within in many different capacities along the way. The most amazing part being that Chris Squire himself asked me to take his spot and keep the ship sailing, along with the other members of Yes. And so it shall be done – for Chris, the fans and quite frankly my undying passion for the band and the music I love do much. Yes means the world to me, and I'm going for it as my dear friend and mentor Chris Squire requested I do.

PRESTON FRAZIER: I got to catch your Baltimore, Maryland date for the YEStival. The band seemed to be in full stride on that date, even though it was early on. Dylan Howe was an excellent addition to the band, working very well with Alan White. Will Dylan continue to be involved for #Yes50?

BILLY SHERWOOD: Dylan was a joy to have play with us, as was Jay Schellen. Alan's health has vastly improved now, and I believe it may just be him on the next tour. To be honest, you would have to ask the drum department, with regards to this question.

PRESTON FRAZIER: You have been extremely busy outside of Yes, with the Circa album in 2016 and then the revival of World Trade in 2017. Tell us about juggling those projects.

BILLY SHERWOOD: [World Trade guitarist] Bruce Gowdy and I set off to writing the *Unify* record, and about 2 months later we had all the songs. We then spent a few months recording. My memory is a little fuzzy as to exact time lines, but it happened quickly, relatively speaking.

PRESTON FRAZIER: What is your set up for the #Yes50 tour?

BILLY SHERWOOD: I endorse Spector basses, Tech 21 amps, TC Electronics, Behringer consoles, Rotosound strings – and I'm working on a Starbucks endorsement. [Laughs.]

2. Additional Interview: co-host of the Yes Music Podcast Mark Anthony K

Welcome Mark Anthony K to discuss the 1980 Yes album 'Drama'. Mark is co-host of the Yes Music Podcast and band leader of the Prog-Metal band, Projekt Gemineye as well as co-leader of the band The Dark Monarchy (2023)

Preston Frazier: I am very fortunate to have Yes expert Marc Anthony K here to talk about one of my favorite Yes albums. This has been kind of a struggle for me as there are a number of albums by the band Yes, which I love, but I think right now this is probably my favorite.

'Drama' is the tenth album by the band 'Yes". It came out in 1980, and it really is unique among Yes canon in that it is the first album by this lineup. Now, some would say it's the only album by this line-up, though they released 'Fly from Her-Return Trip', a rerecording of the original 'Fly from Here', but that's another story, which we'll get into one other day.

Mark, my understanding is Yes were planning to get together in 1979 in Paris to do another album after Tormato, and that fell apart. Rick Wakeman left and Jon Anderson left, and the remainder of the Band, Chris Squire, Steve Howe and Alan White invited Geoff Downes and Trevor Horn from the Bungles to join the band.

Most people would never think that combination of musicians, Downes, Horn, Chris Squire, Steve Howe and Alan White would work together, but in my mind it did. And, Mark, I don't think this is your favorite Yes. I think your favorite is Relayer….

Mark Anthony K: That's correct. 'Relayer' is my favorite Yes album, hands down, but Drama has much to offer. Some of the Yes die-hards, the '5% for something' fans initially were very critical of the album.

When it first came out, people are kind of shocked by the whole thing. Many said, "Oh, my God, no Jon Anderson! How can this be Yes?!"

I think now, years and years later, it really has received more stature.

The album has an interesting foundation. There was even a period after the 'Drama tour' after the Buggles left the band when they announced a tour that was just going to just include White, Howe and Squire, and they're going to play with some other musicians then at the end of the show, they were going to do a bit of the 'Drama' album.

I think people got really excited about that.

That tour never materialized and the band went their separate ways Over the years, the album has gained in acceptance and popularity.

Preston Frazier: There are a few reasons for the increased popularity of the album over the years. 'Drama' is one of my favorite guitar albums that Yes has done. Steve Howe sounds incredible. He brings out a whole bunch of different sounds. He's aggressive yesterday always tasteful.

He uses his Gibson Les Paul Jr., his Fender Steel, a Telecaster and his hollow-body Gibson ES175. His sounds are aggressive and dirty, as is bass playing by Chris Squire.

Mark Anthony K: Absolutely. He really expanded his use of the guitar. We always think of Steve, as a the ES175 guy even though he has an arsenal of wonderful guitars he's used. The 175 is more often associated with him.

During the recording of 'Drama' he started bringing in a Stratocaster.

He started bringing a Gibson 355 too which was his main guitar when he was in Asia.

All of a sudden Howe discovered distortion before. He kind of was just a very clean player. Maybe for a little solo here and here he might add a little bit of distortion or crunch here and there.

The beginning of "Machine Messiah", I'll never forget that. I thought, "whoa, what am I hearing here?"

That's not an organ, that's a guitar.

He's really crunched up his guitar sound here. What a way to open an album with that song.

Also, the unison lines and harmonized lines that he plays with Geoff Downes are unbelievable!

Preston Frazier: Yeah, that's a good way to start! "Machine Messiah", which, as you mentioned, has this distorted, crunchy sound. Howe's playing his ES175 on that. A jazz hollow body guitar sounding like that?! I love it.

Mark Anthony K: It definitely has an interesting sound, like you said, no one would expect it coming out of that guitar.

What I like about that song in general is just the different landscapes he provides us.

The album and the song have that kind of a guitar, then really nice acoustic guitar sounds in there that just sound fantastic.

He likes to throw a little bit of reverb and stuff like that onto his sounds.

It has such a great attack and then softness and then back in.

Preston Frazier: I read in the Tom Morse book on Yes that the person who wrote most of the music for the song was actually the late Alan White. He came up with that rhythm part and that driving part and then the band kind of built on that.

Mark Anthony K: Alan White. What a big loss in the Yes community. He is such a good songwriter. The song, "In the Presence" from 'Magnification'!

That piano at the beginning. What a beautiful part.

I'm so glad that during the symphonic tour they gave him the little spotlight to come out and play it.

Preston Frazier: I'd be remiss if I didn't talk about the drum sound in this album because it is fantastic.

Eddie Offord was originally brought in to produce and engineer however, he engineered only, the basic tracks. He had some issues and he left and the band brought in Hugh Padgham from the Police and Genesis.

Mark Anthony K: Eddie Offord had a few issues when they were recording the album.

Remember that story about his walking to the sessions with a parrot on his shoulder?

However, he knows how to record Alan.

That's one of the best drum sounds I think I've heard on a Yes album. I mean, sure, people will say, oh, no, 90125 and okay, great. Those are all great album sounds, sounds too. But this sound on this album is fantastic.

Preston Frazier: We didn't talk about the lyrics. All the songs were listed as co-written by the entire band.

Making sure they all had an equal share of royalties. All the lyrics on this song are written by Trevor Horn and he does an amazing job not simulating John Anderson, but really providing a progressive rock type lyrics because we don't quite understand what he's talking about. It seems mystical and moves the song along.

Mark Anthony K: Absolutely. One of the things I like about this record is that we have that element of mysticism but it's not the John Anderson 'what's going on here' way.

These lyrics are left for your interpretation.

The opening song is so essential on a record. It kind of makes the listener either say, okay, I'm excited about what's coming or I don't know if I want to take the needle off now and just put it away.

This is one of those records that for sure, you just want to keep the needle down all the time through it because it's just a well written.

Preston Frazier: As epics go, it's a wonderful song. This is the only epic on the album. The album is actually pretty short. I think it's about 38 minutes.

"Machine Messiah" kicks it off in grand fashion then we get one of the shortest Yes songs, "Man in a White Car". This song is mostly Geoff Downes who came up with the music and mostly Trevor Horn who came up with all the lyrics.

It's mostly played on a Fairlight CMI keyboard controller synthesizer with a little percussion from Alan.

Mark Anthony K: Yes this song is a sort of interesting interlude.

A little breather in between the next song and the epic opener. Downes comes up with a great sound.

It is a very interesting keyboard with the kind of touchpad controller and computer screen. All the sounds you can make with it. Just unbelievable.

Lyrically the song is about founding bassist Chris Squire.

He's the man in the white car. I don't think I've heard very many songs by bands that talk about a certain member of their band in an album like that. Maybe the Beatles.

The song has little snare rolls and little percussion. It's a little symphony.

Geoff Downes did a great job writing a piece that was catchy, but not overly pompous.

I think this is much more melodic than something like Cans and Brahms from 'Fragile'; much more well-structured, and it has vocals, which I always kind of prefer than just a strictly instrumental piece.

Preston Frazier: I remember seeing Yes on a Topographical Drama tour. I guess was 2017 or so and Geoff Downes had a bank of nine keyboards, really just playing two of them at this time and getting the sounds from the 'Drama' album.

There is a slightly longer version, on a deluxe edition of 'Drama', but it works for what it is.

Alan White contributes play percussion in terms of marimba. And Alan was great at different types of hand percussion and tune percussion.

The next song is "Does It Really Happen", which is one of the hardest rocking songs on the album and was written mostly by Chris Squire, I believe it was written around the time of the Paris sessions.

It is also one of the weird ones on this album, where there are no guitar solos.

Mark Anthony K: Yes, there's no guitar solo! There are lots of little intricate little lead lines and stuff like that, but there isn't a proper solo in this song.

But you know what?

Do you really miss it?

The song is so well written and constructed.

The bass sound your full attention immediately.

Preston Frazier: I don't know what kind of bass he plays on this. I'm not sure if it's Rickenbacker or what, but it is so prominent. He gets such a great bass sound this album.

Mark Anthony K: It's definitely one of those songs that I really enjoy. One of the things I found interesting about the structure of the song is where just when you think it's done, it comes roaring back in and surprises the listener.

What a great arrangement trick to put into a song.

Preston Frazier: It's another song with prominent Hammond B3 organ by Geoff Downes.

He doesn't play like Rick Wakeman, but it's still there in a supporting role and it sounds great. You have the marimba again from Alan White. You have those nice lead guitar lines by Steve Howe and you have another song where the harmony vocals by Squire are just as prominent as a lead vocal. It all works.

Mark Anthony K: The fantastic harmony vocals on this album stand out. Especially when considering the band doesn't have Jon Anderson.

The absence of Anderson, one of the notable voices of progressive rock music on a record could be seen as a blow but Trevor Horn does a great job on here, and as long you have Chris Squire's voice on a record, you're going to be doing fine. He has such a great voice One of my favorite records is 'Fish out of Water' and, I mean, he's just singing that all by himself.

Preston Frazier: Next up is "Into the Lens" which is a redo of The Buggles song "I Am a Camera".

The majority of the song was by Trevor Horn with harmonies by Chris Squire. Howe plays his Fender Telecaster and a Fender steel guitar lead and solo. The song also marks the first appearance on this album of the vocoder by Geoff Downes.

Mark Anthony K: The vocoder is something we never got when Rick Wakeman was in the band.

Geoff deserves credit for introducing it to the band. The vocoder is something that's very unique and it was very of that time period.

Sound and textures, are really important. The band was facing criticism for being musical/rock dinosaurs so keeping on top of sounds like this help a band stay out of that sort of bracket of being the old guard.

Preston Frazier: He hit it right on the head because first of all, the keyboard sounds sound modern.

Downes is a different player than Wakeman or Patrick Moraz. There are no twiddley bits or fluff in terms of his keyboard playing. The guitars on this album more aggressive, and the drumming is nuanced and powerful. Chris Squire's bass parts are equally aggressive. The album has some of his best playing. The songs are not all short. They're pretty meaty songs,

The arrangements are really well done.

Compared to 'Heaven and Earth' where they didn't have really tight arrangements, they didn't really work through the sound, they didn't get the drums right, and the guitars were really not up to snuff. In terms of the mix. It seems like two different bands. In some ways it really is.

Mark Anthony K: I think that it's very well written in terms of pacing of the songs, the song sequence and the sound.

"Into The Lens" has an interesting vocal interplay with Horn, Squire and Downes' vocoder.

The song also has those little guitar lines which are just great. They are so Steve Howe! Howe's guitar work on the entire album has such a deep melodic structure.

Preston Frazier: That's interesting too because Howe did not record his guitar parts with the band. At least his lead and solos. He did that totally separate in a separate studio. It's probably second or third time in a Yes history he's done that, where he's taken the time to be away from the band and do his guitar work.

He did that with again with Anderson, Bruford, Wakeman, Howe, where he didn't go to Montserrat, he did his parts in London. Regardless of how his parts were recorded for 'Drama', the guitar is seamless.

The next song, which is Run Through the Light" is equally fascinating. It also features fretless bass playing by Trevor Horn, who's an accomplished bass player. My understanding is Chris Squire encouraged Horn to play the fretless bass over the weird time signatures. And then you have Steve Howe playing his red Les Paul Jr. and Chris Squire, I believe, playing a clavinet keyboard, not a piano.

Mark Anthony K: This is one of the rare times on a Yes album, where Chris Squire is not playing a bass on a song.

Preston Frazier: Yes, not counting the ABW&H songs from 'Union' and the song, "The More We Live- Let's Go".

Mark Anthony K: Squire not playing on "Run Through The Light" took people by surprise.

The band was focused on the premise what's good for this song is what should happen.

Preston Frazier: That brings us to the final song, which is probably one of the more popular songs in this album because they've played it a number of times since John Anderson left the band starting with Benoit David's tenure, "Tempus Fugit"

Mark Anthony K: The song is very 80's Yes!

"I've Seen All Good People" has that 70's Yes vibe. It's all peace and love.

"Tempus Fugit" has an aggressive almost punk energy.

What a great song.

The interplay between the guitar and the keyboards is jaunty and aggressive.

They just play this brilliantly.

Preston Frazier: Chris Squire's bass part is amazing, so driving. It's almost manic how he plays it. And it's perfect in terms of precision, but it's hard rocking. Howe's playing on his Stratocaster is equally powerful and aggressive.

Mark Anthony K: This is one of those times where Squire pulled out that bass, I think it's an 8-string one, that has that internal effect system, where he can get a flanging effect and delays. That flanger phaser sound is so prominent.

It's just so trademarkish for Chris Squire.

I remember when I had Billy Sherwood played on my Projekt Gemineye album, 'In The Years 3073 book 2', I asked him to play on the instrumental and he gave me two tracks.

He said, he had a track of him playing without many effects, but he also has one which he called his Chris Squire sound.

It was very similar to the "Tempus Fugit" sound. It has stereo spread and kind of phasing, chorusy sound on it. And of course, I use that on the record!

Not many bass players have that sound which is instantly identifiable like what Squire had.

Preston Frazier: "Tempus Fugit" is one of my favorite Yes songs. One of the things that really drew me into Yes was I'm a big Toto fan Yes and Toto toured together but Chris Squire got sick. I knew Billy Sherwood through Toto because he wrote a few songs with them.

I got tickets to see them three times, on that tour. Squire unfortunately died right before the tour started. I remember them playing, the song but I thought the tempo was a little bit off from

Alan those nights I saw the band. But it was great to hear it. It's great that this song has stayed in their set list for a while.

"Does It Really Happen" And also, of course, "Machine Messiah" have been in their set a few times.

Mark Anthony K: It's too bad this lineup was better received. There were already sold out dates for Madison Square Garden on that tour. The North American fans were in shock when the 'new' band took the stage.